I0633363

Travis, Texas is the third in a series of historical fiction about the old West not long after the Civil War. Gary Harmon writes a factual, yet entertaining book about the growth of a small Texas cattle town called Travis and its development in the 1880s. The town becomes filled with unique characters from renegade Comanche Indians lurking in the shadows, to the town drunk, to the dentist cum Lutheran minister, to the young couple trying to keep their ranch viable on the edge of the frontier. Harmon has poured hours of research into his books to make them historically accurate and the reader comes to realize that much has been left out of our school textbooks: from the plight of women after the Civil War with the loss of so many men, to the problems encountered trying to develop a ranch with "wild" Indians hoping to destroy the white settlement. Gary also makes clear why the hate of the Indian toward the white man has been well-earned. In the old West life, was full of challenges, fear, disappointment and death. Gary knows much of what he writes—he grew up on midwestern ranch and adjoining stockyard so he knows first-hand the tough life of a cowhand and the struggles involved in living off the land.

—Barbra Northup

OTHER BOOKS BY GARY HARMON

The Broken Spur (Drinian Press, Huron, Ohio 2016)

Amber's Place (Drinian Press, Huron, Ohio 2019)

BIRD DOG PUBLISHING

TRAVIS, TEXAS

GARY HARMON

BIRD DOG PUBLISHING
HURON, OHIO

Copyright © 2022
Gary Harmon and Bird Dog Publishing
All rights reserved.
This book, or parts thereof, may not be reproduced in any
form without permission from the publisher; exceptions
are made for brief excerpts used in published reviews.
ISBN: 978-1-947504-35-6
Bird Dog Publishing
PO Box 425, Huron, OH 44839
Lsmithdog@aol.com
http://smithdocs.net

Credits:
General Editor: Susanna Sharp-Schwacke
Copy Editor: Larry Smith
Cover & Layout Design: Susanna Sharp-Schwacke

ACKNOWLEDGEMENTS
For C.J. and Cassie

Thanks to my Saddle Pals:
Mary Jane Anderson
Barbra Northup
Tamara Barker
Mark Koch
Pat Tomazic

And the folks at Bird Dog Publishing:
Larry Smith and Susanna Sharp-Schwacke

AUTHOR'S NOTE:
Thanks to everyone and anyone who
helped me tell the story of Travis.
If I have forgotten anyone, I am sorry.

DEDICATION

This volume is dedicated
to the loving memory of
Dona Harmon.
Wife, mother, grandmother, and teacher,
her fingerprints are on every page.
We covered life's trails together for 53 years.
May 7, 1940 - April 25, 2022

PROLOGUE

The late July heat was nearly unbearable to the men and beasts alike of Travis, Texas. The absence of trees or even high brush on the prairie created a dire shortage of shade. All day the heat had pressed upon the land in glassy waves. Fortunately, it was late, and the sun would be setting soon.

Red Stick lay atop a grassy knoll and peered down on the village through battered army field glasses. Fighting the heat, he was stripped of his clothing, save a breechclout of deerskin. As he carefully studied the dimensions of the town below, he pondered deeply about how much suffering these white people had brought to the Comanche.

Indeed, the Comanche were no more. Without horses there could be no Quahadi (Antelope Eaters), no Nocona (the Moving People), no Penatuka (Honey Eaters), or Jupe (Forest People). Once the horses were gone, the fiercest warriors of the plains allowed themselves to be shepherded on foot to the railhead, loaded into cattle cars, and transported to the reservation at Fort Sill, Oklahoma. They marched along, heads down and defeated, as if they were sheep.

Even Quanah Parker, one of the most feared of all Comanche warriors, had surrendered his gun and took to the reservation. But, not all. There were a few who would never surrender. They were called *lobos* and *zorros* by some. Wolves and foxes. Red Stick was one of these. There were others. Even Quanah Parker's mother, Cynthia, had not accepted this defeat.

Cynthia Ann Parker had been taken captive by the Quahadi at age ten and had become a fervent Comanche. Married to Chieftain Peta Nocona, she had taken the name Naduah (The One We Found). She lived as a dedicated Comanche for twenty-four years.

Rescued by Texas Rangers led by Charles Goodnight twice and returned to the white community, she had escaped both times and returned to her beloved Comanche ways and family. Upon learning that her son, Pecos, and daughter, Topsannah (Prairie Flower), had died while they were incarcerated in Oklahoma, and because she would never see them again, Cynthia chose death. In the spring of 1871, in protest, she starved herself. Her son Quanah was the only one of her three children to survive her, and he did so on the reservation.

Red Stick vowed he would forever wage war on the whites he hated. But first, he needed companions. Dog soldiers like himself. As for how many, he would take what he could get. He knew recruitment would be difficult. Further, he knew he could not prevail in open warfare with the whites. They were simply too many. His new tactics must be to use the skills of the night fighter, the guerrilla warrior. The terrorist.

For this, of course, he would need horses. Weapons. As of now, he was poorly armed with a battered U.S. Army Springfield 45-70 single shot. He had three rounds of ammunition left and, to obtain more, would have to involve theft—perhaps murder.

To the south, beyond the settlement laid out before him, was the sprawling cattle empire called the Broken Spur. This was the home of many horses. Guns, too, he reasoned. Red Stick would start his war of terror there.

CHAPTER ONE
Travis, Texas
September 1888

The town of Travis, Texas, named for the hero of the Alamo, had felt no rainfall for the past twenty-four days. Its main street was filled with swirling little dust devils, as the perpetual west wind made its way along the powdered earth of the thoroughfare.

This dry spell was not unusual for September, often the driest and hottest month of the year. On a late Saturday afternoon, as usual, the area cowhands and ranch workers were beginning to drift into the little conclave of businesses that made up the village of Travis.

At the head of Pamela Street, which served as the main artery for travel as well as the town's foremost avenue, stood the blacksmith shop. Here Andrew Caldwell, a powerful, bearded man in a leather apron, surrounded himself daily with the blasting heat and swirling sparks and smoke that emitted from his fiery forge.

The ring of his maul against the anvil's steel sent out a bell-like tone that could be heard to the far end of main street and for several hundred yards out onto the open plain.

Pamela Street was a dusty lane that ran west to east and fronted every building. All of the buildings were located on the street's north side. On the south side was the plain of buffalo and grama grass that stretched as far as the eye could see, until the land gave way to the sky at the horizon.

Juan Garcia called this prairie *la tierra del hombre muerto*. Dead Man's Land. In years long past, the Kiowa and Comanche had named it *Qual Tepo*. Buffalo Blood. Far out into the endless plain the grasslands were divided by the waters of the splendid Canadian River. This fine waterway originates in the Colorado Rockies and flows south and east below the northern panhandle of Texas on its way to the Arkansas.

Though late afternoon, this day was no exception of work for Smithy Caldwell. He had pledged two dozen horseshoes to Juan Garcia, top hand of the Broken Spur Ranch and, without a doubt, his best customer. Caldwell knew it was Garcia's habit to visit the town on Saturday. He generally showed up late and left early, but he usually showed. Andrew vowed the shoes would be ready.

Garcia usually rode into town on his favorite black and white spotted pinto, Diablo. He loved that horse as a companion, and riding was as natural to him as breathing. Caldwell knew, though, that on that day Garcia would be driving the green Studebaker buggy or the flat buckboard to accommodate the weighty load of horseshoes that awaited him.

Separated by a narrow alley from the blacksmith shop was the catalogue store for Montgomery Ward. Here one might order from the concrete canyons of Chicago any number of items ranging from calico dresses to rolled barbed wire, a saddle, or a rifle—the list was endless.

It was Saturday, however, and that meant the store was closed. Although it was traditionally a good shopping day and a hard-working merchant might well make it the best business day of the week, proprietor Israel Greenbaum was a practicing Jew. Greenbaum's would remain closed on Saturdays because that was his sabbath, as it had been for those of his faith for four thousand years

A vacant lot was next. At one time a hardware store had stood there for as long as anyone could remember. For a very long time it was the lone structure, but eventually the settlement of Travis just grew up around it.

Addison Goodman had built the store primarily as a hardware supply depot for the Broken Spur Ranch. With its quarter million acres and more than fifty cowhands at roundup time, the Broken Spur provided the bulk of the Goodman's commerce. It was commonly believed Juan Garcia had fronted Goodman the cash to build the business, about six hundred dollars in Mexican pesos. The rumor was that this money had been gotten during Garcia's early days as the *bandido del Rio Grande*. In time other smaller ranchers had begun to use the store and, after five or six years, the business was providing a generous living to the Goodman family.

Then Goodman's wife, Elenore, passed away. Six years later, Addison himself was kicked by a horse he was shoeing. He lived another three days and passed quietly in his sleep. Their only child, Clem, became the lone supplier of hardware and coal oil within thirty miles on the wild, uninhabited range.

Clem was in his early thirties when Alicia Castro happened along. She was the sole passenger on a four-horse stagecoach heading for Rogers, Texas where she thought she could find her mother and a sister. Alicia had recently been expelled from Amarillo.

That town had requested her absence in very unpleasant terms. At her hearing, tar and feathers had been mentioned as well as a hangman's rope. Her involvement in prostitution coupled with various confidence schemes and robbery were the motivation behind her enforced exile.

The Reverend Moses Turnchild was notably angered and frustrated at her escape from the hangman's noose. He was publicly outraged when he learned she was to suffer only banishment as punishment for her activities. Alicia Castro would provide fodder for his fiery Sunday sermons for many sabbaths to come. It was only after spinet player Sister Weneford Kaufman called his attention to the loss of attendance that had occurred after five weeks of his constant lamenting that he decided to select another sinner to distinguish.

Nonetheless, he made it a point to relay this miscarriage of justice in his weekly vespers column in the area's first newspaper, *The Amarillo Champion*. His claim was that ineffective city government had sent Alicia forth to spread her sinful ways to some other community. Reverend Turnchild' s belief was that God wanted sin stopped, not just put out of sight. He suggested that those who had freed her would one day answer to a higher authority for their participation in the indolent spreading of wickedness.

Stagecoach driver Harley Bullock knew none of this. The township constable at Amarillo had given him twenty dollars and told Harley to take Miss Castro as far as the money would cover at the rate of twelve cents for each mile. Harley had no idea what he would do with her when the money was used up. He couldn't see just dumping her along the road.

"Well," he told himself. "I'll just have to ponder that when the money's gone." Alicia was already pondering that same issue.

Harley pulled his four-span to a halt in front of the Goodman Hardware, Wire and Coal Oil Store. Using a hammer from the coach's tool chest, he hammered a broken link from the lead right-hand singletree. He told his passenger that he was going to the blacksmith shop for a new link or a repair to the old one and that she should remain in the coach.

As Alicia sat and waited for her journey to resume, grateful for an escape from her recent difficulties, she came to the attention of Clem Goodman. He thought he had never seen a lovelier woman.

From his pitcher pump he gathered a gourd dipperful of cold well water, carried it to the coach and offered it to the lovely Alicia. When Bullock appeared with the new harness link and after he installed it in only a minute, he noticed his passenger was missing.

"Miss Castro! Miss Castro!" he shouted loudly. "We got to leave now." In a moment she appeared in the doorway of the hardware store and waved him on.

"I'll be stayin' here," she said.

Silently, Harley Bullock climbed up onto the high coach seat, whistled to his quartet and drove them west on Pamela and out of Travis, leaving Alicia Castro behind and, he presumed, in the arms of Clem Goodman.

Their relationship lasted for three years, but never became the blissful love land that Clem had sought. Their noisy brawls were heard far too often up and down Pamela Street and it was commonplace for Clem to appear before his hardware customers sporting a blackened eye or a split lip.

15

Their clashes were at once noisy and physical. The love-making that accompanied their reconciliations could best be described as savage. They were two angry people, each searching for a thing that was never meant to be.

On several occasions Clem's relatives and friends had advised him to send her on her way, to be rid of her. Clem, though, was spellbound by her beauty, and he believed that sometime in the future there would be happiness for the two of them.

In spite of their herculean brawls, he could never imagine being without her. Fight furiously and then cease fire were the marching orders of the day. He was certain that he loved her and eventually, they would come to terms. He held firm to this belief for nearly three years.

It was a splendid morning in late May when Clem arose from his bed and realized Alicia was gone. So was her old carpetbag, most of her clothes and Clem's Colt revolver. He sat in a cane-bottomed rocker on the hardware store's porch, gazed at the open grassland across Pamela Street, and brooded. He barely spoke to anyone and gave his customers little or no attention, spending most of his days staring at the open plain.

The land was breathtaking and beautiful as only a Texas prairie in the month of May can be. Wildflowers were abundant. Sedges and sage were in full bloom and the meadowlarks called to each other as they sought the locust they so esteemed. Bluebonnets flourished as far as the eye could see and contributed a tint of azure that seemed the very soul of the prairie. A thousand yards out, a scattering of cottonwoods marked the banks of the Canadian River. Hawks and eagles used these few tall perches as ambush sites to aid in their quest for prairie dogs, snakes, and marmots.

Guhl wa pa (Living Water) the Comanche had named the river, the longest branch of the Arkansas. Originating from the Rocky Mountain snow runoff in Colorado and New Mexico, she flows east and south more than nine hundred miles across the whole of the Texas panhandle on the way southeast through Oklahoma and finally to her Arkansas destination. Every trail herd leaving Texas for the Kansas markets of Abilene and Dodge city would eventually have to cross the Canadian.

In the early spring, the river was a roaring flood and only to be crossed by the most daring of souls. After a few years of trial and error, cattlemen learned to plan their drives to reach the Canadian in August or September. These were the dry months of Texas, and the river could be forded easier than any other time of the year.

After one successful August crossing, one cowboy was heard to remark, "Ain't enough water in that ditch to back a two-ounce shot of red eye."

Though Clem stared at the waving grass and the cottonwoods endlessly, they were of little interest to him, and he cared even less about the river. He was only barely aware of its presence. When the second week had passed, Clem finally came to the realization that Alicia was gone and would never return.

Late that night he again found himself unable to sleep. Alicia was crowding his mind. Tears rolled down his cheeks as he thought of her. Of sharing his bed with her. Of hearing her sing as she went about sweeping up the store in the mornings. He missed the aromas from the kitchen, where she fried pork chops, chicken, or bacon. Even when they were fighting, which was often, to Clem she was breathtaking.

There would be no sleep again that night. Exhausted, he rose from his bed. Checking his front and rear doors, he satisfied himself that he had locked himself in the store. He dropped his two keys into the deep well beneath the pitcher pump.

He then spread a gallon of his finest coal oil around the store, and he set the store ablaze. Clem perished along with his daddy's hardware business. What was left was the only vacant lot on Pamela Street, the bare ground that would be coveted by more than one entrepreneur of the day.

Doctor Pritchard's brother, Randall, had penned a petition to Robert Trav asking him to consider assigning the sale of this vacant lot to Randall as the proposed site of a cattleman's and horse trader's bank. Randall had two hundred thousand dollars pledged as initial deposit, mostly from Chicago and Saint Louis meat packers. He deemed this more than enough to handle the opening of a commercial bank in a town the size of Travis.

Next door to the east was George Tully's barber shop. Tully had learned to operate the telegraph keys while serving the Confederate forces during the War Between the States. The tiny barbershop was the best choice, then, for Travis' telegraph office. It served as post office, the Wells Fargo dispatch terminal, and stagecoach station. The arrangement was usually a good one. Tully was a very reliable public servant. Usually.

From time to time his pinto mare, Daisy, would be spotted tied to the cherry tree at the side of the widow Sarah Meadows' house, just two miles east of Travis near the Caney Creek crossing. Those who truly loved their horses were disturbed that the mare would sometimes remain tethered in the same location for as much as two whole days without drink or hay. During this same period, of course, Travis would be without mail, telegraphs, or haircuts.

Next came the constable's office where Tom Arnette, a former cowboy of the Broken Spur, acted as a sheriff appointed by Old Robert Trav, owner of the Broken Spur and originator of the town itself. The very land the town of Travis sat on was, at one time, grassland of the gigantic, sprawling cattle kingdom.

Tom was charged with keeping of the peace in Travis. The job came with a combination office and sleeping room, complete with a cot and basin. It was joined by two ten-by-ten barred jail cells with their own cots and buckets. He also had the respect of every citizen of Travis. Tom Arnette was a quiet and deeply religious man who could be as dangerous as the situation required.

Doctor Pritchard's medical office was next, and then came Gurske's Emporium. The sign above that door declared, "General Merchandise, Hats, Boots, Candy and Notions." When the infrequent town meeting was held, it was either convened in the Travis Trinity Church that sat in a small, separated cluster of buildings several hundred yards east of town or Gurske's store.

Wolfgang Gurske himself was a wily German immigrant who ran his store, traded horses, and bootlegged the lager beer he and his wife brewed in a small shed to the store's rear. No one knew how or why Wolfgang had come to be so far west. Immigrants often stopped and set up their shops far east of Travis. Most German newcomers halted their travels west as soon as they found a piece of land where they could grow a crop, open a store, and build a Lutheran church.

In laying out the town, Old Robert Trav had directed the church and the school should be at least one hundred and fifty yards from the Staghorn saloon which was next in line and the last building on the main corridor.

The saloon was a two-story wooden affair built in the board and batten style. The main floor was a slapdash combination of a drinking man's saloon and a low-limit card room. Four spartan rooms on the second floor were furnished only with cots, one chair each, a basin and pitcher, and a traditional chamber pot. Without even a curtain for the front window the rooms, nevertheless, were occasionally used as hotel rooms for the sporadic drummers who called on the tradesmen of Travis.

Lars Sengstock had envisioned a sort of neighborhood community center when he arranged, through Old Robert's stepson Colin, to build and operate the Staghorn along with Lars' own son, Oliver. Lars had hoped it would be a gathering place for informal town meetings concerning important subjects such as beef and grain markets and politics. Disappointing both Lars and Colin, the tavern had evolved into a loafing place for the town's drunks and ne'er-do-wells.

Nineteen-year-old Oliver Sengstock was fine with everything just the way it was. He swept the floors, emptied cuspidors, and ran errands for anyone who asked. Mostly, he paid close attention when any of the young women of Travis were available to watch. Sometimes this activity became quite blatant and was more than a little disturbing to his father as well as the objects of Oliver's attention.

Lars had resigned himself to the fact that Oliver's only real talent was the playing of his guitar. Self-taught on an inexpensive instrument a Mexican cowboy had left two winters ago in lieu of an eight-dollar bar bill, Oliver could coax even the most complex of melodies from the steel strings of the flat top box.

No one understood where this mysterious talent came from in an otherwise lackluster personality. From plaintive cowboy dirges to the liveliest of square dance tunes, Oliver could "pick 'em out." Regardless, when Oliver picked up his guitar, everyone listening gave him the adoration and attention that he had never experienced before.

Lars had lost his wife to smallpox ten years ago. He loved his son, and in her absence, doted on the boy whenever he could. Oliver so reminded him of Olivia, he often found himself tearful when he imagined he saw her within his son. Somewhere in the back of his mind, though, as he watched his son go about his duties, he couldn't help but wonder what the future held for Oliver.

Old Robert had always thought any town should have at least two saloons. It was his reasoning that if two people found they could not abide one another, they would have a place to drink without suffering each other's company. To date, he had to admit, one drinking establishment had been more than adequate.

The third and quite odd little building in the separate cluster next to the school was painted red with yellow shutters. This colorful addition housed the dental practice of Doctor Marcus Armstrong who, oddly enough, was also the Pastor at Travis Trinity Lutheran Church.

Mary, Queen of Scots and her followers had struggled for more than two hundred years to keep Scotland purely Catholic, only to have the Protestants win. Similar battles for church dominance had taken place all across Europe, most notably in Germany where Martin Luther's movement led to an entire religion being named after him. By the time a very young Robert Trav came to America there were German Lutherans everywhere. Robert's Calvinist Protestantism was easily converted. Therefore, Travis was a Lutheran town.

Burton Cole made a somewhat precarious living by games of chance. A thin man with a pale complexion and a pencil line moustache, he seldom displayed any emotion. He spent his days and a good portion of his evenings within the bare board walls of the Staghorn.

Win or lose, his face was fixed with a perpetual, empty smile. All in all, he was a rather good-natured fellow for a gambler, and he liked nothing better than to ride herd on Old Robert Trav. Any day he could get a rise from the normally stoic cattleman, Cole felt was a good day indeed.

"Get your hairy ass over here to the table, you skinny old rickety bear hunter. I'm looking to take some of that Longhorn money right out of your pockets and into mine."

"You must be forgettin' what took place here last Saturday," Trav answered.

"Hell no, I ain't forgettin'. You was cheatin' me blind. I'm fixin' to get my money back."

"I damn sure don't have to cheat to beat a miserable card player like you. You play like a little girl. If you got any money in your little girly pocketbooky, just get it up here on the tabletop."

The raucous din of the two noisy poker opponents spilled out into the street. As he approached the Staghorn, Juan Garcia knew in a moment it was time for him to see his oldest friend, Robert, back to the Spur.

With only a little coaxing, Garcia convinced Robert that he was tired, a little drunk and far too expert in the art of poker to waste his talents on a low-grade player the likes of Burton Cole.

"*Por favor*, how the hell did you get into town anyway?" Garcia wanted to know.

"I rode the kitchen buckboard," Robert answered. "Walter said the kitchen was out of beans and rice and some other stuff I can't recall. Anyway, he's headin' for town in the buckboard, and I just catched me a ride along with him. I swear to you, Johnny, that's one rough ridin' sumbitch. Bounced my hat off twice."

"Was the boy Oliver around today?" Garcia asked.

"Why sure he was. Ain't he always. I'm tellin' you, Juan, that boy probably wears out a broom a day. He never stops sweepin'."

"Except when a señorita is on the boardwalk."

"Well yeah, there is that. Still, his papa watches him close. I'd guess he's a good boy."

"I don't know what we'd do without Walter in our kitchen," Garcia changed the subject.

"We sure wouldn't eat very damn well…like we do," Robert answered. "Spur grub's the best on the Canadian River."

Garcia wasted not a moment in agreement.

"Si, si. That's *positivo*." he said.

Comforted by the gentle ride of the Studebaker's rubber covered wheels and heavily padded leather seats along with the warmth of the September sun, Old Robert Trav drifted off into the contented sleep of one who knew he was headed home. He was safe in the care of his dearest *compadre* and comforted by the four drams of good Caney Creek whiskey he'd had at the Staghorn.

*   *   *

Home for Robert Trav for many years had been one of the great mysteries of the Texas panhandle country. It was called the big house by the Spur riders, an ostentatious mansion of the highest quality built by a famous Chicago Architect named Henry Hobson Richardson. He was not famous at the time the Spur house was built, but later in life as the designer of railway stations, his name was to become a household word in the world of famous builders. The splendid furnishings were the pride of Chicago's Marshall Fields.

The manse was to sit empty for many years until Robert's stepson, Colin, brought pretty Pamela Carstin and her son, Justin, to the Spur. It seemed that Robert Trav had ordered the big house built with the constant hope that someday Colin would marry and take up residence in it. Although years in coming, at last it had happened.

Old Robert Trav occupied a small, front bedroom on the first floor. Though he had lived in the small wattle and daub cabin that had served as ranch house for more than three decades, he had come to love his present quarters. He had a small and friendly fireplace, and a large front window that looked over the front porch across a grassy lawn and out to the horse corral. Best of all, his door was next to the staircase and only steps from the kitchen and dining room. From here he could catch the noisy comings and goings of his beloved family.

The rest of the home was quarters to Pamela, Colin, Justin (now a strapping twenty-year-old ranch hand who elected to live in the bunkhouse with the other herdsmen a good deal of the time) and Buck, Colin and Pamela's ten-year-old son. Here was a handsome, inquisitive youngster and the apple of his grandfather's eye. The house, barren for so long, was now alive with the sounds of family. Rambunctious and rowdy at times, Robert Trav could not have been happier.

"Colin," Pamela said one mid-morning. "I wish you would stop getting out of bed and out of the house so early every day. I miss some of that early morning cuddling we used to share."

"You know, sweetheart," Colin was pretending to be thoughtful. "You're right! Right as rain. I promise to do better. I'm gonna start right away. You'll see. Tomorrow is a cuddling day."

Pamela sealed the bargain with a sweet smile and a knowing wink. Colin could feel his face flush.

Colin often wondered about the intimacy that he and Pamela shared. It seemed like there was two distinct personalities within the special, intimate time they shared. On the one hand there was the deep, sincere feeling like two people bound together with rawhide thongs forever, being swept along with the fury of a prairie fire. But, on the other hand, and just as prevalent, were the hoots of laughter and the childish giggling of a raucous fun time.

Colin had puzzled over this riddle may times. Which was the attitude he found the most delightful? There was no forthcoming answer. He had at last concluded one without the other was half a load.

Without a doubt, however, he relished thinking about it, stewing it over and over in his mind. He found it delicious. Enticing. The anticipation of what was on the way was a bonus check. One cashed by Colin regularly. He was thinking on it when suddenly Pamela barged her way into his somewhat lascivious deliberations with a problem she had been wrestling with recently.

"I don't know why Justin spends so much time in that old bunkhouse," she declared "He has a fine, private room right here with us. He doesn't even eat with us often anymore."

"He's a cowhand now, Pammy," Colin told her. "He's becoming a man. He wants to be with men. There's some pretty entertainin' man stuff always goin' on down there, you know. Rowdy stuff. Not fit for genteel, pretty little girls."

"I haven't been a genteel, pretty little girl in a long time. I used to be one, afore I started takin' up with the likes of you. I think I'm going down there sometime, anyhow. I'd really like to know what's going on in that old shack."

"Why, I think that's a wonderful idea, Pam." Colin agreed. He affected a sly smile. "There are about six, seven good young men down there. Hard-working, honest boys. But I got to tell you—they're also rowdy, tough, and vulgar. Go down there and nose around a little. You might could learn how to roll a cigarette. Dip snuff maybe. Catch a cheater at the card table, or you could learn to castrate a bull. Maybe they'll invite you to join in one of their after supper fartin' contests."

He stood and adjusted his belt. "You could show them how to let one of them ladylike windies. You know. Never makes a sound but'll burn your eyes. When you see 'em fetch out a ruler they're about to start one of their manhood contests. You won't be able to enter that contest, but I'd bet it'll be fun for you to watch."

Pamela's cheeks suddenly went crimson. A tiny flicker flashed through eyes that had to have been anger. She turned on her heel and stalked from the room. As she passed through the door, he thought he heard her in a low voice say, "Fuck you, Colin."

Stunned at first, it only took Colin a moment to re-alize he was mistaken as to what he thought he had heard. Why, Pamela Carstin Trav would never use language like that.

CHAPTER TWO
St. Louis, Missouri
Spring 1888

Lisa Strong and Jesse Taylor were just two of the uncounted casualties of the great Civil War. From 1864 through the turn of the century, hundreds of young women like Lisa and Jesse—young women, alone, without family, and without recourse—had come to rely on dubious skills in a constant game of wits. The war had taken the lives of seven hundred and fifty thousand young men. The number of young single or widowed women left behind was immeasurable. Industry had come to a standstill for lack of operating funds and working men.

Jesse—a willowy, flaxen-haired young lady of seventeen years—could truly best be described as beautiful. When she entered the room at the Evening House, she was the center of attention among the admiring young men. Her features were as though they had been affixed by a sculptor familiar with classic Greek statuary. She wore her hair long, straight and resting on her shoulders. Her blue eyes sparkled with life when she smiled. Her friend Lisa told her often, "Your face should be on a coin."

Lisa—shorter, dark-haired, and perky—was often complimented when told she was "as cute as a bug's ear," a phrase of flattery common to the day. Her hair bobbed shorter than Jesse's, her lips formed a perfect bow and her slightly turned up nose somehow hinted at a sly mischievousness. Unlike Jesse's flashing blue eyes, Lisa's were deep, dark pools of mystery in an otherwise honest and open countenance.

Both served as hostesses at Jacque's Evening House, the largest cabaret establishment on the St. Louis riverfront. The Evening House offered many diversions and forms of entertainment. There were dining and dancing, of course. The main floor of the club presented the best bands of the day, while upstairs was the delightful rowdiness where the ragtime tunes of the day were a staple.

Vaudeville skits were offered along with carnival acts, such as fire-eating and trained animals. Poker, dice, and roulette were some of the busiest activities. In short, from sundown to crack of dawn, the Evening House was the spiciest spot on the Mississippi riverfront with something for every taste.

A featured attraction was the bevy of beautiful young ladies. About a dozen in all were on the scene every night. They functioned in a number of capacities, from serving drinks to dancing with the customers or just sitting at a table talking with men who were expected to tip them generously for their time.

It was true that some of the women who worked there also moonlighted as prostitutes. Indeed, Jesse had resorted to this. But it was only a few times. And then, only when she was extremely hard up for money.

"It's not bad at all," she told Lisa. "If you get a nice fella, it's even fun and the money's nice. You should try it."

Lisa had not tried it and she told herself she would not. There were occasions when her money ran out and she wondered if she would be able to hold to that conviction.

It was easier for Lisa than Jesse, though, because of her unique poker skills. Her main job at the Evening House was to serve as the house's poker player.

Arranged with Jacques Chastain, owner of Evening House, the house took ten percent of every pot. When Lisa won, she got fifteen percent of what was left, and the house would cover her losses. They didn't have to kick in very often. Lisa's poker playing skills were legendary and gamblers who prided themselves on their game came from afar to watch her table and to play against her.

When Lisa lost a hand now and then, it was usually for the purpose of keeping players at the table, thinking they could beat her. She played each hand with her "cute as a bug's ear" smile and no other expression of a good or bad hand that her opponent would be able to read.

When she won and raked in the pot, she seemed almost apologetic that she was taking her opponent's money. When she lost, she would often exclaim, "Well, what should I expect when I take on a player as good as you?" Or flattering words to that effect.

Jesse served drinks and sometimes handled the dice table. A craps table takes no talent on the part of the operator and Jesse was paid five dollars for the evening and was permitted to keep her tips. Most of the hostesses were only to keep half their tips and received no other pay.

Jesse felt fortunate to have a job of any kind. This time in America, these post-Civil War years, were some of the most impoverished the nation had ever experienced. Occasionally, Jesse found herself being encouraged to sing.

Jesse certainly was not without talent. Unpolished, untrained, self-taught, and simply basic, she was nonetheless gifted with an appealing and lilting voice. She, when encouraged, entertained at the club by singing the popular songs of the day. She could play the guitar just well enough to accompany her singing and sometimes she would pick up additional gratuities of a few dollars.

More importantly, it made her happy when people enjoyed her singing. She could bring a little crowd to cheerful exhilaration with her renditions of "Funiculi Funicula" or "Polly Wolly Doodle." Equally, she could have her audience dabbing their eyes as she played and sang "The Empty Cradle" or the "Cowboy's Lament." The sweet sadness of "Aura Lea" made it a favorite of the time.

Lisa and Jesse started to work at the Evening House at about the same time and at once took to each other. In a few short weeks they were very close pals, and within a month they were sharing a two-room suite in the old and very worn Bowie Hotel near the stockyards on unkempt, trash-littered Claremont Street. It was a muddy thoroughfare within the St. Louis meat packing district. As they were unpacking the flour sacks that served as their luggage and setting up their new home, Lisa saw the grip of a pistol protruding from a pocket of Jesse's smock.

"You have a gun?" Lisa was surprised.

"Sure—I got a pistol." Jesse produced a small, nickel-plated revolver with mother-of-pearl grips. "It's my thirty-two," said Jesse, matter-of-factly. "I left home when I was fourteen. Daddy gave me this. He said I might need it sometime. Mostly I forget I even have it. How about you Lisa? Got a gun?"

"No," Lisa answered.

"You ought to get one. Never can tell." With that, she rolled the revolver up in a towel and tucked it beneath the pillow on her bed.

When they were not at the Evening House, they were likely to visit some of the neighboring saloons near their rooms. Being in the stockyard district they would meet cattle men of all kinds. Buyers, sellers, feeders, and cowboys.

As it was with the Evening House clientele, many of these barroom customers wanted a try at Lisa at the poker table. Jesse entertained a select few of these for money back at their hotel rooms, but it was a rare occasion when this happened.

Truthfully, Jesse and Lisa were doing pretty well for themselves. Financial recovery for the nation was slow, and many women of the period turned to desperate measures to survive. The streets and brothels were filled with young women who would never have taken to this lifestyle had another choice been available.

The life that Lisa and Jesse led was far better than those unfortunates consigned to the streets. Of course, their youth and beauty, coupled with Lisa's skill at cards, were largely responsible for their frugal, but comfortable, lifestyle. Older or unattractive women faced some incredibly hard times, sometimes even dying alone in a doorway or darkened alley.

Jacque's Evening House was filled with revelry every night. It seemed to Lisa that the only people in the world that had any money were the drinkers and the gamblers.

They ate one meal a day at the Green Frog Café near the river and carried home foods that required no cooking. Many women in poorer circumstances had become addicted to alcohol or cocaine. These held no appeal for Lisa or Jesse. During the day they shopped in secondhand stores and, occasionally, attended vaudeville matinees at the Bijou Auditorium in the Baden Riverfront area.

On Sundays they went together to morning services at the Mount Zion Lutheran Church. After the service they were likely to walk down to the river docks and have a hearty lunch of catfish fiddlers and hush puppies. A mug of sweetened tea or a stein of beer cooled in the waters of a well generated an elegant afternoon. A later stroll through River Front Park assured the two of a chance meeting of young men who might invite them to supper or to a club for a dance or two. Monday, though, they were back to cards and dice and serving drinks.

In truth this lifestyle, while a long way from perfect, was comfortable enough they were likely to enjoy it for a long time yet to come. It was the killing of Charles Crawford that was to change their lives forever.

The bouncer, Joko, escorted Crawford (known everywhere gamblers assembled as C.C.) to the table attended by Lisa Strong.

"Lisa," he said. "Mister Crawford has asked to be allowed to play poker with you at your table this evening. We have informed him that his limit is one hundred dollars per hand. We are depending on you to keep that limit."

"Sure, I can do that. Good evening, Mister Crawford."

"Please call me C.C.," he said. "Everyone does."

Lisa found herself looking at a thin, handsome man. Dressed impeccably in evening attire, he was a darkly suave man who had earned the reputation of the ultimate high roller of the Ohio and Mississippi riverboat gamblers.

His black hair lay close to his head and was obviously pomaded, and he had a moustache so thin it appeared to be applied by a pencil. He effortlessly glided into a chair opposite Lisa.

"Is it truly your intent to hold me to that childish hundred-dollar limit, Miss Strong?" he asked through a disarming smile.

Lisa returned the smile leaning forward toward him in her "cute as a bug's ear" way. "We all know about you, C.C. The kind of poker you play would bust our bank on your second bet."

"I see. We could play for matches you know."

"Your call. I'm going to beat you anyway."

"Yes, I think you might. Before we play, can we chat for a moment or two, Miss Strong? I've heard so much about you; about your skill as a player."

"Call me Lisa," she replied. "What can I tell you? I'm lucky."

"Lucky, is it? I think we both know that luck does play a role in successful poker gaming. But, there's a lot more to it than that and I'm sure we both know that, too."

He took a cigarette from a silver case and lit it with a tiny black match that he struck against an abrasive edge of the case. He didn't offer Lisa a cigarette because smoking was unpopular for women at this time.

"May I have one?" Lisa was bold. "And a light please." As he held the match for her, she touched his hand. She drew deeply on the roll-up. "What would you care to talk about?" She blew a light cloud of smoke skyward.

"Where did you learn? Who taught you? I suppose you know you're quite famous?"

"My daddy was a sailor," she began. "Lost a leg during the Mobile blockade. After Momma died, he and me—Him and I," she corrected, "were together near all the time. We played poker. Daddy couldn't work, so he played poker every night. He was supposed to get a pension every month, but it just about never came. You're famous for high stakes games. Can you believe it? My daddy played for nickels and dimes. Nobody had much after the war."

"That must have been pretty tough."

"Not really. Not really tough, I mean. Daddy was a real fine player. A good night he'd win six bits or a buck. It was okay. We weren't the only ones who were poor. Civil War took everything. Daddy used to say the war swept over the country like a great storm. When the storm finally passed, we were what was left. We got along, though. Boloney sausage was ten cents a pound. We got eggs for two cents apiece. A half a loaf of uncut bread was a dime. Our landlord had given up asking us for rent. Nobody much wanted our shack anyway. Landlord knew when he got rid of us, his new renters would likely be the same. We only lived two blocks from right here.

"Ain't a great neighborhood, you know. Stockyards was right across the lane. Smells pretty ripe sometimes. So that's how it was. Fried boloney and poker every day. Daddy's leg finally took him and somehow—I'm not exactly sure how—I ended up here. Two years now. I still win one once in a while. Let's play."

"But what did you do? I mean, when your father died?"

"I went and saw this old lady next door. She was always real nice to me. I said to her my daddy has died. What must I do? She said for me to leave him. She said that's what folks do when they have no money.

"You just left him then?"

"Well, I covered him up with our best blanket. I used his warbag and packed up some things I owned. We had a tin box daddy put a little money in when he won some. I had about fourteen dollars. Fourteen dollars all in nickels and dimes." Lisa gave him a smile. "I told him I loved him a whole lot 'fore I left. Found me a room for two dollars a week right near here. I seen people in and out of here every day. I finally come in the back door and asked Joko for a job. I was a waitress for a long time. Till they found out I can play a little bit. That's about all. You ready to play now?"

At the last call of the third game, Lisa had beaten C.C. Crawford two of the three, and the house was up one hundred and thirty-five dollars.

A little over thirteen dollars for me, Lisa mused to herself. *Unless he hits me hard the next game or two.*

Then C.C. excused himself and went to visit one of the four water closets of Evening House. Lisa hoped he would pick one that actually was in working order. Not much improvement in indoor plumbing had happened since 1822, when Boston's Tremont house had installed the nation's first. Even Grover Cleveland found it necessary to keep a plumber on call to serve the first President who enjoyed an indoor waste system. Evening House was no exception. Lisa was just having a sip of her tea and tailoring the deck, when the two ear splitting gunshots reverberated through the club.

"Somehow he knew Crawford was going to be here," Joko explained. He was addressing a small sea of blank faces. "His name's Joseph Cantrell. I guess he lost

36

big to Crawford in a game somewhere. So, he hunted him up. Shot him dead in our crapper. Just too bad for us he found him here."

"What are you getting at?" Jesse was one of six or seven young ladies listening to the bouncer of Evening House explain.

"Anyhow, we're closing up here," Jocko went on. "Our boss Jacques is down in the jailhouse. Sheriff wants to know if he knew this Cantrell fellow. Anyway, till they finish up with all their investigating, the county sheriff said we can't open for business no more." He was elaborating the story, but Jesse and Lisa walked away in a daze.

"I was playing poker with him," Lisa said. "Just two minutes later he's up and dead."

"Don't think on it, Lisa. We've got to think what we're going to do now. Where can we make some money? We're going to have to move pretty fast. I only have ten dollars saved. Well, maybe eleven. There's some change too. Then what? We're broke."

"We're not broke, Jesse." Lisa was struggling.

"Just why ain't we?"

"When the shots…When I heard the gun shots, I ran for the door like everybody else. I raked the table first. I was afraid somebody would take the money if I wasn't there. The house cut was about a hundred and thirty-five dollars. I took his table money, too. Even the ante. We have almost two hundred dollars. I was going to give it back, but who do I give it to? Jacque's is in jail and C.C.'s dead."

"Give it back?" Jesse exploded. "We're on the street, don't you get it? No telling when things are going to change for us." Then after they had walked nearly a city block, "But let me tell you an idea. Now that you're telling me we have a little cash, I'd like you to listen to an idea. My mother's brother, Lars, Lars Sengstock, he owns a famous cabaret down in Texas. My mom used to tell me all about it. They have gambling and follies girls. Big orchestras. Lots of big-time swells. It's a real fine place. I know we can go there, and everything will be fine for us. We can work for my uncle and his son, Ollie. Momma said there's lots of rich men and hardly any girls in Texas. Well, not girls like us anyway. Maybe some little country shit-kickers are out there. No style I'd say. What do you say? Want to go to Texas? Want to see some cowboys? Make some Texas money?"

"Are you sure about all of that, Jesse?"

"He wouldn't lie. He's my uncle. We might even meet some men out there."

"Oh, for heaven's sake, Jesse. We've been around men every night."

"I don't mean the kind of men I've been consortin' with. You wouldn't hook up your wagon to the kind of snakes we been carousing with would you Lisa? The men we know—the ones who come to the Evening House— just live for drinking, gaming and whoring. That's why they come to the Evening House, Lisa, or didn't you know that by now?"

Lisa wanted to be sure her response was not too offensive, but it needed saying. "Well, Jesse, I've seen you cuddle up to more than one or two of those snakes you call them"

"Bet your ass. But it wasn't 'cause I was in love. They had some money. I had none. See. Simple."

Lisa was thoughtful for a moment. "That would be hard for me Jesse. Making love for money."

"It ain't makin' love, you ninny. It's called screwin'.
You make a little cash and sometimes the bed doings are
pretty good, too. Either way, I win."

Lisa felt she had to ask. "But aren't you scared? I
mean—you don't know these men. I'd be scared to death."

Jesse thought for a long time. Their walk had carried them near the river docks and the sounds of a boat
whistle punctuated the air. A horse-drawn cart overflowing
with bottles, cardboard and other refuse driven by an aged,
heavily bewhiskered man directly ahead of them caught
her attention. After a moment of studying the man, she
answered.

"So—What's new about that? Folks like us are
scared all the time anyway. Scared of the police. Of being
robbed—mugged—raped even. You remember Carla?"
Lisa nodded. She did recall Carla. Very young. Fourteen?
Maybe fifteen.

"She had nine dollars." Jesse went on. "Showed it
to me. Said her rent was six dollars a week and she was so
glad she had three extra lousy bucks left over for a change.
Some bastard killed her. Robbed her and killed her for nine
dollars. Left her body in a doorway on Chester Street."

"I didn't know that." Lisa was visibly shaken. "Jesse—
Do you really do this thing? I mean do it often?" The dray
cart and the old man were just turning the corner and Jesse
studied them until they were out of sight.

"Twice. I've done it twice. I may do it again sometime if I need the money badly enough. I ain't saying it's
easy. Sure, I'm scared. How could I not be? Scared of being cold and hungry. Scared of dying in some alley where
the rats can find you. And these men we meet—Always
going to do something for us. Something good. Something

39

wonderful. Except it's never really for us. Is it Lisa? It's just more crap to be scared of."

Lisa nodded in agreement.

"I recall you said to me one time that your father compared the war with a huge storm that rolled across the land leaving nothing but destruction behind. He was right, Lisa. I had never thought about it that way until you told me what your father said. You and me, we're the leavins'. If that storm had not hit, you and me might be sittin' on a porch somewhere. Sippin' lemonade and watchin' our babies playin' in the yard. 'Stead of that, here we are. Scared? Damn right I'm scared. You should be too."

Now a stray alley cat crossed their path. Jesse found herself wondering, *Has that cat ever had a home? Was it ever somebody's cat?* A moments reflection and then she added, "Do you know what we are, Lisa? What we really are? We're the uprooted trees the storm left behind. We're the houses with the roofs blown away. Debris they call it. Leftovers. You and me, Lisa. And a thousand others just like us. Not for that storm we would not be here. Doin' what we are. Bein' who we are. It was the war. The storm that gave birth to us. Made us like this. Here we are. Children of the storm. We got to be tough, Lisa. Ain't nobody going to look after us. Nobody to say, 'Don't touch the stove. It's hot. Stay off the street at night. It's dangerous.' We got to make it on our own. We ain't gonna get no help. Now, how about it, girl?"

Lisa swallowed. Hard. She thought, *Is there anything else? Any other choice?*

"Want to go to Texas?" Jesse was exuberant now. "See some country? Mayhaps get cuddled up by a cowboy? A cattle baron? A real man. A man whose ain't like those we've been hangin' round about. Somebody who really works. Gets dirty. Sweaty. Smells like his horse. So tired come evenings he just wants to sit on the porch and have me sing to him. Then eat a big supper. Tell the kids a scary tale about wild Indians and horse thieves afore pullin' me into a big old featherbed bed right alongside of him. Sound good, Lisa? Is it worth a try?"

"Just where in the state of Texas is this hot spot?"

"I ain't exactly certain where on the map it is—It's in a big city though. It's called Travis."

CHAPTER THREE
TRAVIS, TEXAS
July 1888

The days were long, and the work was hard, but Justin Carstin loved every minute of it. It started when the roundup ended. Cowboys had searched every nook and cranny of the vast Broken Spur lands for the months of April, May, and June, looking for new crop calves that were weaned from their mothers and any unbranded mavericks that had escaped last year's gathering. All these would be driven to a spot just south of the main house called the big corral, where the serious ranching work would begin.

A fenced area of about two acres held the bawling herd while cowboys worked among them. Young bulls were roped, and their heads were held by Juan Garcia's lariat from the back of his favorite roper. A bulldogger then twisted the calf's head and neck to lay him on the ground.

At that point, Long John Barlow hurried from the branding fire with the hot iron, dull red and grey and smoking. With a light touch, he set the Spurs brand on the left hip of the bawling calf. Two wavy marks. One above the other. They represented the Canadian River and were known far and wide as the brand of the Broken Spur.

For the bull calves, Lemuel Sweet dropped to his knees alongside the dogy and, using a razor-edged pocket-knife, split the calf's scrotum with a single cut. He removed the two testes and tossed them into a waiting bucket. Even in late September, flies could be a major problem and so the wounded scrotum was smeared with a black, tarry paste called Screw Worm Smear. If horns were removed by the hacksaw, this same balm would be applied to the horn stub. This effective veterinary ointment would be used during castrations and dehorning's for many decades to come.

When the bucket was filled with bull testes one of the ranch hands would exchange it for an empty container and take the filled vessel to the ranch kitchen and Walter Beasley. These were a favorite food of the cowboys and Walter was a master of the dish's preparation. The cowboys called them Rocky Mountain oysters. Beef fries was the name Walter preferred.

Walter Beasley was a hardened, profane man. Forged in the fiery furnace of the Civil War, he was best described as a tough and cynical loner. Given to chewing tobacco and cursing in the vilest language, it was hard to imagine the gentle regards he had for Old Robert.

Once the Civil War had ended, Walter's Alabama homestead was gone forever. Given away to freed slaves, the Beasleys' fifty-year tenancy of the Montgomery homestead was forfeit to the nation's new restoration program as a penalty for having fought for the South, as well as flying the stars and bars.

When Robert Trav discovered Walter, the ragged Confederate was attempting to snag a catfish or two from the Canadian River to avert starvation. Walter's ragged appearance betrayed his pitiful condition.

"I got me a little farm up the stream a bit and I'm needin' a hand," Robert said. "Tell me, can you cook? I mean cook for a few hungry men. I swear we're down to eatin' jackrabbits and black berries."

"I'm a mighty cook," Walter lied. "Just give me a kitchen to work in and a cot to sleep on and I'll fatten your ass to a fare-thee-well."

Walter very often thought of that meeting thirty years before. He loved Old Robert. Loved him for the life he had given to Walter. For the old man's sense of fair play and honor. Walter was not alone. Many of the Spur hands had come from just such backgrounds. The post-Civil War years found hundreds of such men adrift, impoverished, displaced and lonely. A few fortunate of these had become cowhands for the Broken Spur.

If horns were present, they were sawed away. With the recent presence of Shorthorn and Polled Hereford bulls, the dangerous scimitars of the old Longhorn were not nearly as present as in the past.

Heifers were roped and branded, too. Garcia would spend all day in the saddle, roping one after another and pulling them to the branders. At the other end of the corral, Justin Carstin would be carrying out the same duties.

"Why's his name Carstin, when he's Colin Trav's son?" Wiley Small, a new member of the Spur's cadre, wanted to know.

"'Cause Colin's his stepdad," Long John explained. "His real daddy was killed by horse thieves afore Miss Pamela and Boss Colin hitched up. Better get your ass over to the fires and kick in some wood 'stead of frettin' over such matters."

In a separate corral a mile away, Bobby Baxter was bossing a gang handlining the horse corral in much the same way. Mares and foals were rounded up and corralled so the young stallions could be castrated, turned into geldings. Stud horses were far too unreliable and even dangerous. Geldings and mares made up the working stock of the Spurs range. Only the best stallions were reserved for breeding stock.

The two-year-olds were then tamed a bit by introduction to saddle and a brief breaking ride. This was administered by Bobby. Aside from Juan Garcia, Baxter was the best horseman of the bunch. A colt judged riding age and size would be roped and snubbed to a post in the corral's center.

One of the workers would then blindfold the *cayuse* with a gunnysack. A saddle would be cinched onto the animal, Baxter would climb into the leather and the blindfold would be whisked away. What followed was one of the classic scenes of the Old West like no other.

Pitching and bucking, running wildly into fences and rearing—even falling—only the most determined bronco buster could expect to keep his seat. Baxter was, indeed, one of the very best. For all of his talent he would occasionally taste the dust. He would remount and ride the Texas tornado until the bucking and pitching stopped. When the horse stood winded, with his head lowered and ears forward, Bobby would dismount, uncinch the saddle and ready himself for the next tryst with a cyclone. Ears forward was the sign of a spent horse.

The ridden horse following this exercise was, by no means, a saddle-broken mount. Indeed, the next few times saddled, the rider would have some more of that same wildness to deal with. But the horse was, by now at least, introduced to the job he would be doing in the future.

A few more wild rides and the Broken Spur would have another fine cow horse in the remuda. Juan Garcia was very proud of Bobby, and he had every right to be. Bobby was his discovery and had proven himself over and over, until he had become one of the most important employees of the largest ranch on the Canadian.

Little Bobby Baxter was all of fourteen when he had simply been told by his father that the family could no longer feed him and still survive. With his mother, little sister and baby Ruth facing an oncoming winter, Bobby was informed that there was no way they all could survive.

His father had summoned him to the hog pen and pointed to two thin, half-grown shoats. The two small hogs stared balefully at the pair assessing them. It was obvious they hoped it was feeding time.

"That's what we got till spring to make it on. Them and the rabbits and squirrels I can shoot. You can see they ain't ready to butcher, but I got to anyway on account of I ain't got no corn left. Well, 'ceptin' that what we got to grind for mush and cornbread."

The family, including Bobby himself, had agreed that since he was oldest, the time had come when he must find another place to land. Early winter was still more than a month away and that was to his advantage. To wait longer would almost assure disaster.

His mother had stood in the doorway of the rude sod shanty and waved goodbye, as his father turned away the terrified boy with frightened eyes. A pitiful sight with his little poke of corn dodgers and a few apples, the boy had almost starved out on the plains. Twice he was nearly detected by the Comanches, or maybe they were Kiowa, he wasn't sure. No matter. Both were deadly enemies.

Robert Conrad Baxter had been terrified, cold, and hungry when he finally made it to the Canadian River. It was there Juan Garcia discovered the frightened child huddling under a hedge apple tree and, after a good deal of coaxing and promising the boy no harm would befall him, Garcia escorted the boy to his new home, the Broken Spur. The bond between Garcia and Bobby Baxter would never be broken.

After two solid weeks of their back-breaking labor, the cowboys were finally given a few days of rest. It was on one of these days off and just after a Walter Beasley breakfast of biscuits, bacon, stewed apples and strong Arbuckle's chicory coffee, that Baxter and Justin were sitting on a bench in front of their bunkhouse smoking hand-rolled.

"This here's a Wednesday, ain't it," Baxter said.

"Guess so," Justin replied.

"Know what happens on Wednesday, do you?"

"Damn sure do! Stagecoach day!"

"You up for it?"

"Just need to saddle up. You get ready. I'm whuppin' your ass today for sure."

"You beat Rocket and I'm buyin' beer."

"Just what I need—got me a terrible thirst. 'Sides that, I'm sure my big black's gonna be the first horse on the Canadian River to whup up on old Rocket. High time, too."

"Don't get mad at me when Rocket farts in your face. His ass is all you're gonna see. Maybe some dust if'n it don't settle afore you come along."

It was a ritual these two herdsmen enjoyed every Wednesday when not working. The only stagecoach to serve Travis, Texas arrived on Wednesday afternoon. Baxter and Justin would ride out for three or four miles east of town and then race the coach and each other in a headlong duel of horse and rider, right into the center of town.

On this particular afternoon, as they lined up on opposite sides of the coach and readied themselves for the run, they each saw something they were just not prepared for. On the side of the coach Justin had selected, a lovely face appeared in the coach's window. Justin found himself staring into the bright blue eyes of stagecoach passenger, Jesse Taylor.

At the same moment, on the coach's opposite side, Bobby Baxter was greeted by the smiling countenance of dark-eyed Lisa Strong. A race was about to begin that the four of them would never forget. Even the stage driver was aware something was about to take place, something quite familiar and yet special.

"Whip 'em up Harley!" Justin Carstin called out. "Let's run for it, you old bastard!"

Teamster Harley Bullock looked forward to this race as much as the pair of daredevils at either side of his coach. He whistled to the four-horse team of the day, cracked his long whip once and the race was on. The two lovely passengers within the Wells Fargo carriage were in for the roughest, most frightening, disheveling ride of their lives.

The contest was a wild one. Lisa and Jesse were bounced around like dolls made of rubber as Harley lashed the four-horse span into a whirlwind of thundering hooves and flying manes and tails. Instantly the coach's interior was filled with a formidable cloud of dust from the road.

Flailing about like two beans in a jar, from time to time as they were jostled alongside one of the coach's windows Jesse or Lisa would catch an instant glimpse of the beaming faces of daredevil equestrians.

Lisa, to steady herself before she was thrown from the coach, at last got her right arm out the window and curled it around the door post. Jesse, fighting for any semblance of balance, succeeded in wrapping her arms around Lisa's neck. As the coach flew over the rutted roadway at breakneck speed, all the two girls could manage was to stay erect.

"You son of a bitch!" Jesse yelled at driver Harley through the lung-filling dust. "When we stop, I'm fixin' to kill you!" Justin Carstin heard this threat over the rumble of the coach and the thrash of the flying hooves.

"Whip 'em up, Harley!" he called, laughing. "You ain't no gooder'n dead meat when she gets her hands on you!"

The last two miles of the contest were a melee of winged horses, shouts of the three contenders and the anguished cries of the knocked-about passengers trapped inside the nearly airborne coach.

Relief for the pair was indescribable when, at last, they heard the driver call a halt the team.

"Whoa! Hold up there, Billy. Whoa, Tony. Whoa, Ladybug. Ho, now, Nell." As the team began to slow at last with the jingle of trace chains and the snorting of fired up horseflesh, Harley Bullock finally pulled his coursers to a halt in front of Israel Greenbaum's store in a cloud of road powder.

Still mounted, Bobby Baxter stuck his head into the window of the coach. With an irascible smile, he asked the dust-covered and tousled duet, "Y'all ladies got any bags what needs a carryin'?"

*　　*　　*

Colin Trav was tying his horse, Buck, to the hitching rail in front of the big house, when he was hailed by Wind Walker. Shuffling towards Colin was an old Indian dressed in a black slouch hat and an old blue chambray shirt buttoned tight at the collar. He wore patched, denim trousers faded to near white. His long snow-white hair was shoulder length and cascaded from beneath the ancient, black Stetson. About his neck he wore the remnant of a striped tie. Once a Kiowa war chief, he was now the Little Mary of the Broken Spur. Little Mary was the name given to the dishwasher, wood gatherer and general handler of the ranch's most menial chores.

"Mister Trav! Mister Trav! Old Mister Robert wantin' to see you. He's in the big room with Mister Chester. He say if I see you, I send you straight away to him. Mighty 'portant, Mister Trav. Mighty 'portant."

"All right, Windy. I'm on my way."

Colin, somewhat troubled, climbed the front steps and entered the hallway. It was not like Chet Garret to show up at the big house. He was in charge of the hunting crew and spent his time in the outer regions of the Spur searching for strays and newborn calves. He usually was only around the ranch's center during round-up or trail drives. A true outdoorsman he was perfect for the job.

A big drive *was* on the docket for a pasture move, but that was more than a month away. Colin could not avoid it. He smelled trouble.

"'Mornin', Collie. Come on in here," Old Robert said, calling Colin in from the hall. "Chet's in here. Got some hard news I'm afraid."

50

"Hello, Chet. Been a while since we met up."

"Mornin', Mister Colin. Things goin' bad up by the big spring. Old Wetherspoon gone and got hisself kilt last night."

Colin was saddened immediately.

Amon Wetherspoon had been born into slavery and had lived more than twenty years as the personal property of Henry Clay, the statesman from Tennessee. Clay was a devout slaver who, implausibly, had maintained that slavery was evil and had, by a codicil in his will, freed his sixty slaves upon his death in 1850. Wetherspoon was one of these.

He was as good-natured as any man could be and worked as hard or harder than any cowboy on the Spur, despite his advanced age.

Being free proved for many ex-slaves to be a harsh prison of its own. With no experience of totally caring for himself, Wetherspoon's liberty became an aimless odyssey of wandering, begging, and foraging just to stay alive. Drifting west on foot after the Civil War, he had somehow landed on the doorstep of the Broken Spur. Here, met by Juan Garcia, he asked if there might be a job available.

"Can you ride?" Garcia wanted to know.

"Ain't sure. I never been on no horse. I can sure try."

That was nearly twenty years ago. Since then, Old Wetherspoon, as he was called, had ridden hundreds of miles in search of strays along with Chester Garret's hunting party. His advanced age being apparent, he was often asked just how old he was by the inquisitive cowboys.

"I ain't rightly sure," he'd answer. "But, I'se a great big boy when Jesus Christ was borned." His answer always brought good natured laughter to the hard-working crew he lived and worked with.

A good man. We're going to miss him, Colin thought.

"Accident?" Colin wanted to know.

"More like murder, Mister Trav. Probably a Comanche murder."

"Murder?" Colin was amazed. "For God's sake, tell me what happened. Been no Indians 'round here in a long time."

"Me and the boys had about thirty mavericks bunched up," Chester Garret began his tale. "We headed them up to the big spring. Lots o' water and some late grass left up there. Old Wetherspoon, he goes out on nighthawk ridin' a little sorrel mare. Next morning Cletus had a little breakfast cooked up. Me and the boys are eating a few biscuits and some bacon, and this little mare shows up and walks right into the camp, just as big as you please."

"Only'est thing is, she's alone. We saddle up and light out to find him. When we do, he's dead. Kilt with a tammyhawk in the back of the neck. Been scalped, too. Rifle gone. Part of the broke reins laying on the ground. Simon, he says who what kilt him tried to steal his horse. Probably grabbed at the reins. Old bridle, I reckon. The reins broke and the sorrel jerked away and run off. My guess is Comanche on foot kilt him for the horse."

"Tomahawk, you say?" Old Robert asked.

"Well, little thin axe of some kind. Cut right through the neck bone. Had to have been throwed. Throwed real hard. I don't reckon a man on foot could have reached his neck or head, mounted as he were. I think the axe was thrown by someone who knew how. Scalped him, too. Reckon killer's madder'n hell when he lost the mare. Seems likely Wetherspoon must have heard somethin'. Took out his rifle. Never got a shot, I'm thinking. White men can't throw no hatchet like that. Least ways, I don't think they can. In the dark too. True enough there was some moon but still...."

"Where's Mister Wetherspoon now?" Colin asked.

"On the flat wagon out by the corral. We wrapped him up in his blankets. Didn't know what else to do, so we brought him here. Is there anything else I can do, sir? I need to be getting back to my boys."

"No, Chet," Colin replied. "You can head on back. We'll take care of him now. You got a gun, Chet? You and your boys better start packin' some iron. Be careful out there."

"Got my pistol and belt on the saddle. I ain't leavin' 'em for a minute."

"Don't be afraid to shoot," Old Robert added. "This looks like the work of a lone man on foot. That don't mean they ain't some more of 'em about though."

Chester Garret, assuming the conversation was finished, headed for the door, then turned with an after-thought.

"You might tell Mister Garcia that me and the boys found three more of those old-time Longhorns. Two dry cows and a real old curly-faced bull. I know he wants those old timers looked after, so I'm taking them up to the High Meadow when I get back. I got some others grassin' up there already. 'Bout twelve or thirteen, I think."

Colin was thoughtful. Garcia loved those old Long-horns. He wanted them preserved. They reminded him of the long-ago time when they were the only cattle here.

Garcia loved old Wetherspoon, too, Colin thought. *They've cut a lot of trails together.*

"Collie," Old Robert was deeply saddened, "get hold of Long John. Have him get some boys to put Wetherspoon in the ranch cemetery near the river. He'd like that, don't you think?"

"I'm sure he would, Papa." Colin grew thoughtful. "What do you think, Papa? Is this just a single happenin'? Or should we be on the lookout for more trouble?"

"Spent most of my young days among red men, Colin. They ain't easily dissuaded. I think you ought to tell all our hands to start packin' a gun everywhere they go. If they ain't got a gun, you ought to get 'em one. We got to see to it that Pammy and Little Buck are looked after. Justin, too. He's all over the place every day. He's more likely to run into trouble than any of us. I got a feelin' we'll see more of this horse thief. I 'spect he ain't done just yet."

Walter knew the "boys", as he called them—though some were years older than himself—had worked extremely hard that day in the corrals. Branding and dehorning calves along with the marking of the young bulls. Walter had participated in corral work before he became the permanent cook of the Broken Spur, so he was sharply aware of the grueling effort. He had readied a massive evening meal for the exhausted workers.

Antelope stew was Walter's signature dish and this evening he had prepared it richer with more of the sweet antelope flesh than usual. His side dishes were bacon-laced cornbread, roasted turnips, and heaps of sliced potatoes fried in bacon drippings. The final course was persimmon pudding topped by the rich, light tan cream from the two jersey cows the ranch hands milked twice daily.

The meal ended; the hands of the spur relaxed about the grounds of the big house. Smoking and talking, planning to enjoy the sunset before hitting the bunks. Long John Barlow strode about the little scattered social gatherings until he located Wiley Smart. When he found him near the little barn where the milk cows and laying hens were housed, he walked up and spoke to him.

"Wiley, I'd like a word with you."

Wiley bristled, recalling the sharp words from Long John that morning when he had asked about Justin having the last name of Carstin instead of Trav.

"I'm right here Long John. What're you needin'?"

Long John dropped his hand-rolled butt to the earth and ground it out with the toe of his boot.

"Wiley," he said slowly. "I spoke a little snappy at you this morning down in the corral. I'm hoping I didn't offend you too much."

"Nope. Not at all Mister Barlow. Had you really offended me—why I'd a just give you a good ass whippin'."

"Wiley." Long John took a deep breath to keep his temper from flaring. "Wiley, you couldn't whip me on your best day and I'm pretty sure you know it. Let's just leave that a while and try to get to the fact that I'm apologizin' to you. Tryin' to anyhow. It's just that you were starting to ask about the bosses here. We hear the same questions from every new hand we hire. I'm the first to admit—Old Robert, Juan Garcia, Colin Trav and Miss Pamela, Justin Carstin and Little Buck—well, they *are* a mysterious batch. I cain't blame you for askin' about them. I'd also say I don't mind tellin' you what I know. Just not when we're brandin' calves."

"Oh, hells bells, Barlow. I wasn't mad. You were right. I should've been gatherin' up some wood for the brandin' fires."

Wiley moved to the door of the little milking shed and sat down on the bench beside the entrance. He fished in his vest pockets until he found the makings and began to build a smoke. Without another word Long John flopped down beside him.

"Well, the way I get it, this whole thing started more'n forty years ago. Old Robert and the Mex. They was the ones what put it all together. Afore they put a claim on this land it just belonged to the Comanche and the Kiowa. Nothin' here but wild Indians, buffalo, and coyotes. Was you to ask Old Robert where was it he come from he's probably gonna say he was from Scotland but that he weren't no Catholic."

"Scotland? Catholic? What's one thing got to do with the other?" Wiley wanted to know.

"I ain't too sure my own self." Long John was trying to pick his words now. "Way he tell, it was this old queen named Mary way back in time wanted nobody to be a Protestant. If you was, she had your head cut off."

"Damn! Them's hard doins. Seems to me some of them religious folks of a real long time ago was pretty damn strict. Crazy maybe." Wiley allowed.

"Yeah. Reckon some still are," Long John agreed. "Anyhow he sailed to America from Scotland when he was about twelve or thirteen years old. He was gonna be a fur trapper and I guess he was for a long time. He said to me he was at one time on the Niagara River then all around the Great Lakes. Hit a trail south to the Ohio River country. That's where he jined up with some trappers headed for the Rocky Mountains."

"Damn! He's been all the way to the Rocks?" Wiley Smart was hearing the tale of a saga he could only imagine.

"Garcia said he lived with a Crow woman for a while. Says he's still lovin' her. Never took no other woman. I reckon with all his money, his wherewithal, he could likely have got another had he wanted. Garcia said he never once even tried. Loved his Crow squaw. Still does, I imagine."

Wiley Smart was enthralled. It was truly a rags-to-riches tale and he loved hearing it.

"What about Mister Garcia? Where does he fit in?" Wiley wanted to know.

"I can't tell the whole thing 'cause I don't know it all. I can tell you Juan deserted the Mexican army and was a highwayman for a long time."

"Highwayman?"

"Robber. Stick up bandit. The bandido of the Rio, he was called. Mexican police, Texas rangers—all were after his scalp. Mister Robert found him out on the plain all shot to hell. He patched him up and got him all healed up and they been together ever since. In the old days they had to fight hard to hold onto this land. They stood shoulder to shoulder and took on all comers. Did you ever see that little cemetery over by the river?"

"Matter of fact, I did see it. I walked over there one day. Counted twenty headstones."

Long John stood and Wiley figured he was nearing the end of the story.

"More folks than twenty over there. Garcia says some of them were so lowdown he refused to mark their grave. Now, there's one more thing I want you to know about. That's Miss Pamela. We call her Miss, but make no mistake, she's as married to Colin as anyone ever was married. She and her first husband and the boy Justin set out for this part of the world with a string of Kentucky racehorses.

They figured on breeding them to good wild horse range stock. Figured they'd get a special kind of horse that way.

"I reckon if you don't know it, racehorses is the craziest sumbitches you likely to ever see. Bred to run fast and turn left and that's about all they know. Now, Pamela and her first husband—Alex I think—they figured if you had all that speed and could couple it with the brains of a horse that can survive in the wild for hundreds of years you might really have somethin'. Horse thieves killed her husband and when Colin found her and the boy they was about on their last legs. They made it here and been together ever since. If you look at the east pasture, you'll see a few of the horses Miss Pamela has bred. Texas quarter horses she calls 'em."

"Oh, sure, I saw those. I was gonna ask about them. They sure are a fine-looking string," Wiley allowed. "Quarter horse? What's a quarter horse?"

"Racehorses," Long John replied. "Fastest horse ever for a quarter mile. Got wild horse brains bred into 'em, too, Faster than a lightning bolt and gentle as a barn cat. Ain't no cow can outrun 'em or out smart 'em. Best cow ponies ever bred. They's cowboy smart. Good for ropin', cuttin', herdin'. Just name it. I'm gonna sure be glad when she has enough stock to mount all the Spur riders."

It was at that moment Walter interrupted their discussion with a shout from the back door of the cook house.

"Hey there, Long John…Wiley. I got some puddin' left over. You don't want it I'm a throwin' it."

"How's that sound to you Wiley?" Long John asked.

Wiley stood and scratched his bottom.

"Reckon we'd best handle that puddin' I think."
"Yep. I'se thinkin' that too."

CHAPTER FOUR

Travis, Texas
July 1888

Jesse and Lisa sat together in one of the four travelers' rooms on the second floor of the Staghorn Saloon. Hot all day but now, as sundown approached, the room had cooled a bit. They sat side by side on one of the cots provided for itinerant salesmen hawking their wares to the merchants of Travis. They had dragged a second cot into the room.

The two looked out of the window down onto the dusty main street and south out onto the endless prairie. The street was deserted now, the Travis residents having headed indoors for thr evening as the day came to a close. A sense of sadness and dejection filled the darkening room.

"Oh Lisa," Jesse was near tears, "how can I ever tell you how sorry I am. All his letters—All my folks told me. I truly thought my Uncle Lars was—was—well more than this. I'm so sorry I talked you into coming here."

"Just hush, Jesse," Lisa replied.

"I'm just so sorry I—well, I expected a large cabaret, like the one in Saint Louis. Orchestras and dancing. Not this—this shit house in the middle of nowhere. It's a two-bit beer joint in the pits of hell!"

"I'm sure we'll work this out somehow. Your Uncle Lars seems pretty nice."

"Yes, he does. But, how about that son of his? That Oliver? For Christ sake, he was looking right through my clothes! Made my skin crawl just lookin' at him. I've seen some horny bastards in my day, but—Oh Lisa, what a mess I've made."

"Stop. You don't need to tell me you're sorry. I know you are. I'm not mad nor angry with you."

"But, you're so quiet. I thought you were hating me."

Lisa took a moment with this. "No, not angry. Sure not hating. Just thinking. We're here. No money to leave. At least, not yet. We can't just lay down and die. I've been trying to figure out just what we *can* do."

"And?" Jesse asked. "I'm so glad you ain't mad with me."

"Jesse—You thought your uncle Lars was a big success and you offered to share your good luck with me. How could I be mad? You're my pal. We're here together and we'll figure out how to leave here together. Let's just sleep on it. Tomorrow's another day."

"Golly, I love you, Lisa. I'm gonna be okay. You know why I'm gonna be okay? 'Cause I'm with you, that's why... I wish we had something to eat, though. Just a little hungry."

"That'll be first thing we work on tomorrow. Let's just rest now."

The sun had given up trying. No question, the day ahead was to be cloudy and yielding to a drizzling rain. While Lisa and Jesse may have found the gloom and damp somewhat depressing, the rest of the citizens of Travis were in a celebratory mood, as the first rainfall in more than three weeks settled the dust, relieved the heat and watered the prairie surrounding Travis.

"I'm wishin' this sumbitch lasts all day," Lars Sengstock told son Oliver. "We gonna sell some spirits today, boy."

It reliably worked the same on any inclement day. If the weather was too foul for outdoor work, too much rain, too much snow, or too much wind, cowboys, farmers and horse wranglers would line the bar at the Staghorn.

The poker tables would be alive with action. Oliver would play his guitar to enhance the jovial mood, while collecting a good day's wages in tips. All in all, Lars readied himself for an exhausting, but lucrative, day.

Lisa called to Jesse through the early morning dimness. "Hey there—sleepy head. I've got something for you." She carried a small wooden tray with an assortment of cups and saucers.

Jesse stretched and yawned and fought against the effort of waking. "What's going on? What do you have there?"

"Could I interest you in some coffee?"

"Coffee? You have coffee? Real honest to goodness coffee? Oh my God, Lisa. Coffee! I was just dreaming about coffee. Oh! What are those delicious looking things next to the cup? My Lord, are those biscuits? Real biscuits?"

"They are indeed biscuits. Loaded with butter and blackberry jam. It's good jam, but I'm sorry about the seeds."

"Seeds!? I love seeds! My Lord, Lisa, I've never been so hungry—not ever! Where did you come up with this, this banquet? This feast?"

"Downstairs. Lars and Oliver are having breakfast in a room in the back. When I asked them where I could buy some breakfast, they said I could have some of theirs. You know why, Jesse? 'Cause there's no place to buy breakfast or any other food in this whole town. Big back room off the bar. I didn't even know it was there. I'm there getting this coffee and looking around. You know what, Jesse? It's a big kitchen!"

"A kitchen?"

"Stove, pitcher pump, worktable. The whole works. Lars told me when it rains, they work hard. They were eating breakfast getting ready for a good day. They gave me the coffee and biscuits. They said all the range hands came in to drink and play cards and only left when they had to eat. I got an idea, Jesse. We—you and me—we need to talk to your uncle today. We might be in better shape than we thought. Oh, I'm sorry that coffee's black. It's all they had."

"Black!? I love black coffee. Gimme one of those biscuits!"

At two o'clock in the afternoon, while the rain was still steadily falling, Lisa decided the time for her pitch was as right as it was ever likely to be. The Staghorn Saloon was jammed to overflowing with drovers from everywhere within ten miles of Pamela Street.

The card tables were filled with players. Other would-be players were standing behind them waiting for an empty seat. Lisa noticed disdainfully that the game of the day was mostly low-limit poker. One large table she observed was wastefully occupied by penny ante players.

The gambler, Burton Cole, was winning steadily from his incompetent competitors. But the pots were small, and he was only raking in forty or fifty cents at a time. Try as he may to raise the limits, he found no takers. These were drovers with a rainy day off. They were only interested in killing time and visiting pals.

Ten cent steins of beer and quarter shots were keeping Lars working at a feverish pace, however. Wine was sometimes requested, and homemade scuppernong was served in a four-ounce gill for a dime. The place was a cacophony of laughter and good-natured cajoling.

Cowboys were laughing and talking of bad horses and good riders, pretty girls they had once known, old folks left behind and pushing wild cattle across the Canadian.

"Looks like a bonanza for you, Lars," Lisa smiled.

"Yeah. Good day. Real good day. This rain is good for the whole country. Me too! It'll last till they get hungry enough to go home." Lars was pumping beer into water glasses and tin cups as every one of his steins was already in use. His remark was more than Lisa could have hoped for. He had opened the very conversation that she had been wondering how she would approach with him.

"If you had a little food for these hard drinkers, you could probably keep them here till closing time. Have you ever thought about some baloney sandwiches? A pot of chili maybe? Stew?"

"Girl! Are you crazy? Loco or something? Can't you see how busy I am? Would you suppose I had time to fix chili?"

"Where's Oliver?" Lisa asked.

"Hidin' out somewheres. When there's a lot of work to do, I ain't never able to find him. But, I can tell you one thing for sure. I ain't for eatin' no chili that Oliver had any hand in makin'."

"Lars, you just keep pumpin' that beer. I want to talk with you about a few things, but that'll keep till tomorrow. How about I give you a hand? I've been a waitress before."

The next day, when the rain had stopped and the crowd was gone, Lisa asked Lars, Oliver and Jesse to join her at one of the card tables. It was time for Lars to hear her proposition.

Tom Arnette had once been a top hand on the spread of the Broken Spur. Since he had been appointed as a type of sheriff by Old Robert Trav and charged with keeping peace in the town of Travis, he had not visited his old job site. Colin was pleasantly surprised to see him heading up the lane, driving a single-seat cart being drawn along by one of Pamela's Morgan horses.

When Sherrif Arnette's cart came to a halt, Colin hailed him. "Gettin' too old for the saddle are you, Tom? First time I ever saw you in a sulky."

"Oh, I can still horseback it, Colin. Fact is this here gelding I bought from your wife is just such a pleasure to chum around with, I just look for excuses to spend some time with him."

"Can't you ride him?" Colin asked. "Morgans are pretty good saddle horses too, you know?"

"True enough. But a cart ride on a day like this is something I don't get to do very often. We like to race these local farmers and their trotters and pacers. Since my Tony don't look like a racer, they all want to try him when we meet along the road. Tony puts on a little kick, and they get the dust. Never breaks stride neither. He's just one heck of a horse."

"Well get to it, Tom. You here for a visit or is there somethin' to talk about?"

"Both, Collie. I'm always glad to spend a minute or two with you, but there's something been troubling me I'd like to speak with you about."

"So, are you just spendin' a minute or are you sheriffin'?"

"Well, it's about all these guns your boys are packin' around town. Your hands been comin' to town for a long time, peaceable as housecats, and then all of a sudden they're showin' up armed like grizzly bear hunters. I'd appreciate you tellin' me what's that all about. I know a man's got a right to pack a pistol, but I also know if you get a gun or two too many on the street, trouble's a comin.'"

"Tom, do you remember Old Wetherspoon?"

"Sure, Collie. I know Old Wetherspoon. I haven't seen him in a long while. I like him. He's a good old feller."

"Well, he's dead."

"Oh, no!" Arnette was visibly shaken. "What did he die from? Just old, I'd guess."

"Killed. Murdered. Horse thief. Comanche maybe. Killed him with a tomahawk, then scalped him. Either an Indian or someone tryin' to look like an Indian. We told our boys to fetch along some iron till we find this here killer."

"Why didn't you report this killin' to me, Colin? I *am* the law you know."

Colin was thoughtful. "I reckon you're right, Tom. We should have brought this right to you. I guess we've just got used to handling things by ourselves for so long, we've forgotten what we ought to have done. Truly, Tom, I apologize for the oversight. You are the law, and we should have come to you. But, about the guns. This outlaw ain't been caught yet. And I don't want to lose another man. You got to remember, Tom, our boys ride in pretty rough country. Alone, too. Sometimes they only got themselves to rely on. There ain't no law up west of the big spring."

"I hear you, Colin. But, Pamela Street right through the heart of Travis ain't all that rough."

"Sorry, Tom. The guns stay till we catch this horse thief."

"So, when you do catch up with him—You're planning to bring him to me, right? Bring him into the jail?"

"You got my word, Tom. When we get him. And we will. When we get him, you can have what's left of him."

Realizing the futility of his efforts, Tom Arnette clucked to the gelding, touched him with the whip and moved away at a hard trot. It was obvious that the Trav family was still the boss of the Broken Spur *and* Travis.

The meeting between Lisa and Lars proved very successful. Lars had known for a long time that the Staghorn should do better financially than it had. He had confidence in these two young ladies who had worked in the large bars of Saint Louis. Lars readily agreed to give fair trial to the changes that Lisa had suggested.

First, the eight-ounce beer steins were discarded in favor of new ten-ounce schooners. The price escalated from ten cents to twenty. When Lisa explained that Lars would be making ten extra cents for two more ounces of beer, he understood the mathematics right away. Israel Greenbaum would provide these new drinking vessels through his Montgomery Ward catalog store.

"Customers will be happier, too," she explained. "We'll put up a sign advertising our new 'Giant Saint Louis Schooners'. No more steins or mugs. We'll sell more beer at a better profit."

"No more free card tables," she went on. "If you want to play cards in the Horn, a table costs one dollar an hour. No more penny ante poker either. No games allowed below a quarter limit. Pennies on a poker table are ridiculous."

On Saturday night, Jesse would entertain by singing and playing her guitar. She would be paid three dollars by the house and allowed to keep fifty percent of the bucket tips. Oliver would provide wood for the cookstove, and Lisa and Jesse would make pots of chili, sometimes chicken and dumplings. They would have baloney sandwiches available for a dime. A baloney sandwich could be served raw, fried or pickled. Boiled eggs were a nickel apiece. Then Lisa suggested she would play poker for the house.

"I never thought about havin' a poker player for the house," Lars said. "Tellin' the truth, I didn't know there was such a thing. Are you really good enough to make money for the bar? For me?"

"She played for the biggest place in Saint Louis, Lars," Jesse injected. She wasn't sure Jacque's Evening House was the biggest, but she knew Lars wasn't sure either. "Players came from everywhere to play her. She's famous on the river—Mississippi, not Canadian."

"How does it work?" Lars asked

"I keep a third of what I win," Lisa said. "You get the rest. You pay my antes and my losses."

"But the boys that play here don't play for very much money. I'm wondering if, with these new limits and no penny games, anybody will come at all."

"That's true," Lisa answered. "Your loafers will quit you. We'll attract some higher-class shooters. I'll lose a game now and then, but in the end—Well, you just have to take the risk to find out."

Lars was thinking.

"How do I know for sure you can play that good?" he asked.

"Tell you what, Lars. I have enough money left to stake myself in a game or two, if I'm careful. You pick the player and I'll try him head-to-head."

"How about Burton?" he asked. "Would you play Burton Cole a hand or two?"

The bargain was set. Lisa would play Burton Cole five hands of draw poker to see if she was who she professed to be at the gaming table. After five hands, Lisa had won four and taken Cole for twenty dollars.

"Gawd damn," Cole complained. "She ain't a card sharp, she's a fuckin' mind reader. She knew what I was thinkin' every damned card."

That very night Lisa Strong became the lady poker player for the Staghorn Saloon.

The changes that took place at the Horn also spread into the community. A different clientele started coming around for sandwiches and chili. Lisa never took to the table till after eight at night. Previously, the bar was starting to empty out about then.

Now, however, a group of more serious players began to drift in. For the most part they were strangers Lars had never seen before. Some came to head up their own game and some to play the pretty lady who played so well. Lars wasn't sure where they came from, but come they did.

The change in Saturday nights, though, was the strangest of all. The women of the town had never stepped a foot into the Staghorn, or any tavern. Now, their husbands brought them to hear the pretty lady from Saint Louis sing and play her guitar.

Shortly after Jesse began to sing, Oliver brought out his guitar and started to play along with her. Since his playing was so much better than hers, they decided to keep the duet and together they made a kind of magic music never before heard in this wild country.

Oliver loved being around Jesse. The guitar playing afforded him the perfect excuse. Jesse complained to Lisa that Oliver's eyes were constantly fixed upon her.

The stairs to their second story rooms presented another problem. The staircase to the upper rooms above the Staghorn was attached to the outside of the building on the east side. It was a steep climb and the two girls joked and called themselves the climbing roses of Travis, Texas. The entire stair seemed to have been shoddily constructed by an amateur carpenter. Or more likely by a cowboy who was no carpenter at all. From time to time the pair wondered if the steps might not just pull entirely away from the building's east wall.

The third step from the top had an audible squeak. Jesse and Lisa would hear the noise from time to time, and wondered if Oliver might be on the stairs attempting to eavesdrop. The sound of that stair step was a sure sign someone was about.

Another major change at the Staghorn that was more apparent to Jesse and Lisa than anyone else was the frequency of the presence of Bobby Baxter and Justin Carstin. While it was plain that Baxter was attracted to Lisa, the feelings that Justin had for Jesse were far more evident. At any time, these two cowboys were not at work on the Spur, they could be found at the Staghorn.

"I ain't sure I can eat anymore baloney," Baxter complained one day, as the two rode into town.

"Let's go for the chili today then," Justin encouraged his friend. "Hurry up, slowpoke." He touched his spur to the flank of his big black. The horse lunged forward at breakneck speed.

"Get 'em, Rocket," Bobby bellowed. And another horse race was on.

It was easy to see Walter Beasley was angered, as he stopped Juan Garcia on his way to the corral. "Mister Garcia, sir. I need you to help me out on somethin'."

"What can I do for you, Walter?"

"It's them damned thievin' cowboys, sir. Come right into my kitchen last night, they did. Stole a whole side of bacon and some bread loaves I was coolin'. Took the bakin' pans and all."

"What can I do about that?" Garcia wanted to know.

"You let 'em know I got me a shotgun loaded up with rock salt and if'n I catch any of 'em in my kitchen again, I'm blisterin' their asses."

"Just take it easy, Walter. I'll speak to the boys. Don't you go shooting anybody, though. Even with salt." It was at that moment Long John Barlow approached the two. He was on horseback and held two metal loaf pans in his hand.

"Look here, Walter. Ain't these two of your bread pans?" Long John asked.

"Sure as hell are!" Walter exploded. "What you doin' with 'em? You been prowlin' my kitchen, Long John?"

"How did you come by those?" Garcia asked.

"Found 'em just layin' on the ground west of the big spring. Somebody had a cold camp up there. No fire, but lots of tracks. Some raw bacon, too."

Garcia took command immediately "Get three or four men together, Long John. I want you to show me where this place is. Bring guns along too. This bacon thief could be the lobo that killed old Wetherspoon."

CHAPTER FIVE
Travis, Texas
July and August 1888

Cletus Garrett had only one dream in his life. His sole ambition since he was a boy had been to be a preacher. He separated ministers, pastors, parsons, and reverends from preachers. They were too tame, he felt, to really express the words of God with the proper emotion. A preacher with a fiery disposition in the pulpit was, in his opinion, the only messenger of God and Jesus that could save an otherwise doomed sinner. He so longed to be that messenger.

For the time being though, he was the trail cook for his Uncle Chester Garrett's hunting party. It was the duty of Chester's party of four or five of the toughest and most hardened of the Spur's men to constantly patrol the distant edges of the Broken Spur in search of stray or unbranded cattle or horses.

Additionally, they were the ranch's protection against cattle rustlers. These men lived most of their lives in the out-of-doors. Only when weather became unbearably dangerous were they driven inside of one of the numerous line shacks that dotted the Spur's perimeter. It was Cletus' job to see that these hardy men were fed and properly coffeed. He assumed the additional responsibility of caring for the souls of his work mates.

"He's your nephew," Lemuel Sweet complained. "Can't you get him to shut the hell up? We're sure tired of them sermons every time we come in to eat. We ain't against him sayin' a prayer afore we eat neither. But he's so damned long-winded, we ain't had a hot meal yet!"

Chester Garrett's rules for his workers were simple. "If it's on four feet and if it's on our land, branded or not, it belongs to us. If you come across a settler or an Indian what's kilt one of our calves 'cause he's hungry, look the other way. If you catch 'em with three or four bunched up, send 'em to hell. That's why you're packin' that gun. It ain't for shootin' rabbits." His only other rule was "Don't bring me no bitching about Cletus 'less you want to take over the cookin'."

The happiest day in Cletus' life was the day he learned that the Reverend Marcus Armstrong had married the widow Morgana Caldwell, the blacksmith Andrew Caldwell's sister-in-law. He would soon be resigning as pastor of the Travis Trinity Lutheran Church and making arrangements to leave Travis and go to Indiana. There, it was rumored, Morgana's family had considerable holdings.

Cletus wasted not a moment. He hurried to his Uncle Chester and pleaded for the day off, so that he might ride into Travis and apply for the position. As he rode the six miles into Travis, he practiced all of the Bible verses he could recall. He prayed for guidance and the Lord's help in obtaining the job, and finished up the last mile or so by singing "Rock of Ages" at the top of his lungs.

The two new young women who worked at the Staghorn had completely captured the hearts of the two cowboys. Bobby Baxter could never get enough of just looking at Lisa Strong. Her dark hair, her pert features and lilting laughter were on his mind each day as he rode among the cattle. Each night as he slept in his bunk. She was ever-present as he went about his day-to-day routine.

Justin's feeling for the singer Jesse may have been even stronger than Bobby's for her friend. Both were strongly encouraged, as the two young women seemed willing to reciprocate their feelings.

Lisa was favorably impressed by Bobby's compact and muscular build. She liked his sandy hair and found his freckled face open and honest. He was impressive in his calfskin vest and batwing chaps. The black Stetson he wore was given to him as winner of first place in the bucking horse competition in an area rodeo. He exuded an air of a man of self-reliance.

Jesse liked everything about this cowboy called Justin. From his shock of sun-colored hair to the bluest eyes she had ever seen and the sun-tanned face of the out-doorsman. He was taller than Bobby and made to look even thinner than he truly was by tight fitting riding pants and black shirt. Both wore spurred boots and had the sage smell of the open prairie about them. Somehow, they were more manly, more virile than the young men she and Lisa had known back in Saint Louis.

When Justin and Bobby learned the girls were off on Sundays, they wasted not one second in inviting them to go for a buggy ride the very next. one Both agreed, but only after church. And so, it was arranged. They would call for the young ladies in the four-seat buggy and the matched team of Morgans. The four would attend church together and later Justin and Bobby would show them some of the surrounding country. All agreed that it sounded ideal.

"I'll get Walter to fix us up some grub," Justin said. "We can eat up by the big spring. You'll like it up there, it's beautiful. It's up pretty high. You can look down and see the river for miles. It looks like a silver ribbon cuttin' through the prairie."

The Sunday buggy rides became a regular occurrence. The townsfolk grew quite accustomed to seeing the foursome leave the church service and drive the Morgans down Pamela Street, out of town towards the river and the prairie.

While the folks of the town thought the foursome were a charming pair of couples, the whole idea was repugnant and upsetting to Oliver Sengstock. He watched them drive the buggy down Pamela Street with rueful eyes. Oliver often had amorous thoughts of himself and Jesse as they played their music together. Now, he viewed the interloper, Justin, with contempt.

This contempt would soon swell into hate. Oliver's disdain for Justin grew, not helped by Justin's obvious wealth and the social position of the Broken Spur family. Oliver recognized that the ownership of a buggy and matched team was far beyond his means.

These Sunday excursions usually included a packed lunch. They often picnicked near the big spring, but Bobby Baxter also knew of some hidden glens along the river. A few of these could provide the luxury of a very private place.

Ranch cook, Walter Beasley, had correctly guessed that Justin and Bobby were sharing the food he packed for them with female companionship, even though they had never said a word to him about it. He looked at it as a time to shine.

He concentrated on packing up the most lavish repasts he was able with the limited grocery list of a ranch cook. Home-canned pickled peaches, vinegar potato salad, roasted ham or turkey slices. Sometimes, stewed chicken with dumplings or roasted beef with a delicious special sauce he had concocted from wild horseradish, crabapples, and homemade pickle relish.

Walter's provisions became a highlight of the buggy trips, and all four travelers were anxious to see what specialties he had provided for the day. After the horses were hobbled and the meal consumed, each couple would announce they were going to take a little walk. Of course, the desire for privacy encouraged them to walk off in separate directions.

Once secluded, the antics of Bobby and Lisa were rather childish and innocent. There was hand holding. A gentle hug or two. A few tender kisses usually followed with each whispering how glad they were for this day and to be together, and an agreement to meet again the next week.

At first the meetings of Jesse and Justin were similar, but on the third such get-together their emotions gave way to a far more fervent display of affection. Fiery kisses. Hugs of quiet desperation. Exploratory hands. The loosening of clothing. And finally, stopping just short of complete lovemaking.

More often than not, it would be Justin who halted the tryst. Both Justin and Jesse sensed there would be a time in the very near future when there would be no stopping.

"I guess I love you, Jesse," he managed to say through difficult breathing.

"I love you too," she replied while putting her skirt back in order. She was glad for the deep glen they were secluded within. She liked the feeling of being alone in the world with only Justin Carstin. What she couldn't know was that from deep in hiding, the Comanche lobo, Red Stick, had watched every moment they were together.

Bobby and Justin were happy and contented as they drove the buggy back to the Broken Spur. It had been a good day. Walter's lunch was wonderful, as usual, and the Morgan's were left to meander as they wished along the road home. Bobby and Justin had each rolled cigarettes, when Bobby noticed Justin was quiet and deep in thought.

"Hey, boy. Where are you?"

"Huh? Oh, I was just thinkin'."

"'Bout what? You're about to over work your brain."

"Bobby, do you remember what Preacher Garrett said this morning?"

"Well, he said an awful lot. What part do you mean?"

Justin took a moment. "The part when the sermon ended—When he said Jesus loves you and wants you to be happy."

"I remember. He says that every Sunday."

"I think—I think he meant me, Bobby. I think he was talkin' just to me."

"Just how do you figure that? I ain't sure I know what your talkin' about."

"What I mean, Bobby, is—Well I'm happy all the time since I met up with Jesse. I think about her all the time and sometimes, when I do, I find out I'm smilin'. Just thinkin' about her and I'm grinning' like a mule eatin' briars. So, I'm thinkin'...I'm thinkin' Jesus wants me to be happy. I'm thinkin' he sent Jesse to me. Jesus loves me and wants me to be happy and so he gave me Jesse. Do you think I'm right, Bobby? Am I happy 'cause of Jesus wantin' me to be?"

"I think you're full of sheep dip. Quit stretchin' your brain."

Pamela Carstin Trav was having her morning coffee on the little balcony outside her second story bedroom. The view here was a pleasant one. She always found it tranquil when that was what she needed. The perch, as she called it, looked out onto the big corral and beyond to the feeding mangers. A pair of blue birds caught her attention, as they flitted about their fencepost nest.

Across the field she could see Long John driving a team hitched to the largest wagon they owned, piled with fresh hay in a mound higher than his head. Using a pitchfork, he was ladling forkfuls of hay into the troughs. A group of four white-faced calves were close on his trail. They were busily feeding behind him as the team pulled him along. She heard Colin enter the bedroom from the hall.

"Come out, Colin. I'm on the perch." She smiled at him. He joined her, drawing a chair and sitting next to her.

"Got any more coffee?" he asked.

"Always," was the reply, as she poured a cupful for him from a sliver service. "Beautiful day, wouldn't you say?"

Colin breathed in a hearty lung full of the morning air, freshened by the smell of the new-mown clover.

"I'll say, day like this one makes you want to just live forever."

"It's lovely here on the perch."

"Best seat in the house," was his reply.

Pamela's mood changed ever so slightly, but Colin still caught it.

"Have you heard our son has a lady friend?"

"Well, talk gets around Travis faster than a west wind. Yeah, I heard that. I guess he's just like his stepdaddy. Always lookin' for a pretty face."

"Did you know she's a saloon girl?" The concern was showing through.

"Oh yes. I heard that, too. To the Travis gossips that's the best part of the story." Colin grew thoughtful. He began to choose his words carefully.

"Have you thought about the last couple of years, Pammy? The things our boy has done? Last year Justin bossed fourteen cowhands and drove two thousand cattle to the rail head in Dodge. He was on the open trail eighty-eight days. He had a shooting run-in with cattle thieves and three different Indian raids. Now the best part: he did all of that with only a four percent herd loss. When he got to Dodge City, he turned down three bids those slick cattle buyers from Chicago offered him. When that first buyer came back to him, Justin quoted him a firm price and sold our herd at the top of the market. He has done this three years in a row. He works hard. He's strong—tough. A lot smarter than I was at his age." Colin finished, sat back in his chair, and sipped at his coffee.

"Why are you telling me this, Colin?"

"'Cause I want you to remember he's one hell of a man. His judgement is as good as anyone's. I'd trust him with my life. Hell, Pam, I'd trust him with *your* life and that's a lot more important to me than my own. If he's fallen for

80

a girl—any girl—I'm betting you there's a lot more to her than just a saloon gal. Whatever anyone says about her, my money's on Justin."

"How did you ever get so wonderous wise?" Pamela was smiling.

"'Cause I married the smartest lady horse trader in Texas. That's how."

Pamela set down her coffee cup. "All this talking has made me a bit tired. Would you like to slip back into bed for a little while?"

"See what I mean? You're pretty dang smart."

CHAPTER SIX
Travis, Texas
August 1888

When the altercation came about in the Staghorn, no one could have been more surprised than Justin Carstin. It was a warm Friday afternoon when Justin rode his big black into Travis with the intention of ordering a few rolls of wire from Israel Greenbaum's catalogue service. It was late in the afternoon and, since it would be after quitting time by the time he got back to the ranch, he decided a cool schooner of beer would be in order after he'd finished with his business.

The bar room was empty except for Lars and his son, Oliver. Lars drew a beer for Justin. Oliver sat at a table strumming his guitar. When he noticed Justin was watching him play, he launched into one of the guitar solos that he played best. When he had finished, Justin complimented him.

"You sure can play good, Ollie. You really are a musician."

"You like my playin' huh?"

"Sure do. That was real fine."

"You know who else likes my playin'? Jesse. She loves to hear me play."

Justin sensed an edge in Oliver's voice.

"I can see why. Anybody would like that song, I would guess."

"Jesse does. You know she'd be *my* lady friend 'stead of you. You know, if you weren't so damn rich. 'Course you bein' so well off don't do nothin' about makin' you smart."

"Oliver, you're about to say too much. Why don't you cap it?"

"Ollie!" Lars spoke up. "Quit lookin' for trouble. Keep quiet!"

"No, Papa. He needs to hear this. You do, too. She's got you both thinkin' she hung the moon. It's just Broken Spur money she's after."

"I think you'd better shut the hell up, Oliver," Justin replied. "You're flat out rilin' me."

"You don't scare me none." Oliver was eyeing the polished walnut grips of the .44 Russian in Justin's waistband. Open topped hip holsters were not permitted for the employees of the Broken Spur.

"Man strutting 'round town with one of them gunfighter rigs buckled on just sends out the wrong kind of a message," Old Robert had contended. "Spur men should always be ready for trouble, but no need to go inviting it."

"I don't care if you got a gun or not," Oliver continued. "I ain't scared of you. You're stupid as shit anyway. Know what I'm talkin' about? I tol' Jesse I'll give her ten dollars to slip into bed with me. Ten dollars! More'n she makes in a week! Know what she says? She says she don't do that no more. You hear that? *No more. She don't do that no more!* She's done it plenty of times before. I'll bet for less than ten dollars, too. She's just a whore and you're just a stupid son of a bitch! Oh, she sure done it a plenty, but now she's tryin' for your money and so—*she don't do that no more!*"

Justin launched himself at Oliver. Fists flying, he tackled him still seated in the chair. The two of them struck the floor, shattering the guitar into splinters. Oliver struck back with a vicious punch at Justin's face, only to catch Justin's fist on his own nose at the same time.

Justin struggled to his feet. Oliver reached inside his shirt and produced a hunting knife with a five-inch gleaming blade. He lunged at Justin, aiming the knife at his chest, but at the last moment Justin turned away from the thrusting blade and caught the blade of the knife hilt deep into his upper arm.

Lars leapt over the bar and ran at his son to stop the onslaught, only to be struck on the temple by Oliver's crashing fist, sending his father reeling and falling in a heap at the foot of the bar. Oliver jerked his knife from Justin's arm and made another lunge. This time he struck Justin just above the belt buckle and, ripping the blade sideways, he cut a deep gash across Justin's belly.

Deeply wounded, Justin fell to the floor. Oliver was again advancing, knife in hand ready to inflict another wound. Only this time Justin pulled the Smith and Wesson revolver from his belt and shot Oliver low in the belly. The report of the heavy caliber pistol confined by the walls of the tavern was deafening. A thick cloud of white gun smoke obscured Justin's vision. Oliver yelled and fell to the barroom floor.

Justin climbed from the floor and onto one of the chairs at a poker table. Taking his neckerchief from around his neck, he held it against his belly wound. Within two minutes of the gunshot, Sheriff Tom Arnette was in the bar. With a moment's assessment he said to Lars, "Go get Doc Pritchard!"

"What about my boy? What about Ollie?"

"He ain't dead. He needs the doc, too. Get out of here, Lars. Get that doctor down here. Now!"

Jesse and Lisa were returning from a special Friday late afternoon prayer meeting at the church.

As they walked along the way to Pamela Street, Jesse queried Lisa, "So, what do you think about the new preacher Cletus compared to our last bible thumper?"

"He's surely not as refined and that's a fact. On the other hand, Jesse, since you've steered me here to Travis, I've come to love cowboy honest. And if Cletus is nothing else, he is that."

"I can't argue with you about that. He still smells like a cowboy. Do you think the congregation will try to buy the old preacher's house? Turn it into a parsonage maybe?"

"That's something to think about."

Burton Cole spotted them coming down the street. As a harbinger of news, he hurriedly caught up with them.

"Big trouble down at the Horn this afternoon," he told them. "Cowboy shot Oliver. Got himself all cut up, though. Lars is pretty mad at you, Jesse. He says all the trouble was your fault."

"Oliver shot?" Jesse asked. "What cowboy? Who shot Oliver?"

Jesse felt her knees give way and she fainted right into Burton Cole's arms when he told her it was Justin Carstin.

*   *   *

"How did I get here?" Justin wanted to know. Forcing himself to awaken, he realized he was in his own room on the second floor of the big house. The bright sunshine pouring in the window that faced to the east told him it was morning.

"Doctor Pritchard brought you, Justin." It was Pamela's voice.

He rolled his head to the direction of the voice and saw his mother sitting alongside the four-poster. To her left sat Colin Trav and Bobby Baxter. The trio wore expressions of anxiety and worry.

"Why?" Justin fought for understanding. "What's happened?"

"You had a fight—over to the Staghorn," Colin told him.

"A real bad fight," Pamela added. Justin blinked his eyes and shook his head. The fog was clearing now.

"I know—I remember. I shot Oliver. I killed Oliver! Oh my God." Justin was distraught.

"Oliver's not dead," Pamela said. "Actually, you ended up hurt worse than him. You're lucky to be alive. If not for Doc Pritchard, you would have left us."

"I ought to go see him. Oliver. I never shot anybody before. I've got to go and see him. Thank God he's not dead. I didn't kill him."

"You're a long way from going anywhere, son," Colin injected. "Your belly wound is a bad one. It'll be a spell afore you can sit a horse. Oliver ain't there any more anyway. At the Staghorn, I mean. Sheriff Arnette went to call on Lars and Oliver. He told them he thought they should move on. Find a new place."

"And they left? Just like that?"

"Well, you know Tom Arnette can have a way about him when he needs to," this from Bobby.

"Yeah, for a religious man, he can be downright scary. Who's running the Horn?"

"Closed. Locked up tight. Key's over at the sheriff's office. At least, for now," Colin said

"What about Jesse? Jesse and Lisa? Where are they? Is Jesse okay?"

"Well," Baxter spoke now. "Lisa's still in her room above the saloon. Garcia told her she could have the room as long as she needed it. I've been sort of lookin' after her."

"Jesse—Where's Jesse?"

"She's gone, Justin."

"Gone? Gone where?"

"We don't know where. She took the stage out of town not long after your fight."

"Why, Bobby? Why would she leave without telling me where she's goin'."

"Well," Baxter measured his word carefully. "She told Lisa that Oliver had told you some things about her past. Things that she intended to tell you herself. Things she hated for you to hear, and she couldn't—she just couldn't bear it. I knew you'd want her back Justin. I searched for her for two days and never found a trace. I know she rode the stage out toward the railhead over in Rogers. Me and Rocket tried to find her, but it was just no go. Lisa said she had no idea where Jesse could have gone, except maybe back east. She told me to tell you Jesse had said to her twenty times how much she loved you. She just couldn't— Oh hell, Justin. I don't know what to say."

"Maybe she'll come back on her own, Justin," Pamela said.

"No—No, she won't." Tears were making it difficult for Justin to speak. "Oliver hurt her pride. Crushed her. I wish I'd killed the son of a bitch."

CHAPTER SEVEN
Travis, Texas
September 1888

Ranch cook, Walter Beasley, was watching from the window of the cookshack as Juan Garcia helped Old Robert from the green buggy and up the front steps of the grandiose mansion that was the main ranch house of the Broken Spur spread. Walter knew instinctively that his boss had spent the day carousing and drinking at the reopened Staghorn, since he had taken him into Travis that very morning.

"Wind Walker! Come here," Garcia commanded.

From around the corner of the house from where he had been watching in a silent vigil came the ancient Indian, anxious to please.

"Put Mister Robert's rig away, Windy. Rub this mare down, too. Give her that quart can half full up of oats. That's the red can. Not the blue one. She's been standing at a hitching post a long time. I had a lot to pick up in town." As he spoke, he was helping Robert wake himself enough to dismount the buggy.

The old Indian did not speak but gave a vigorous nod that told he understood. He caught the horse's bridle at the bit and started toward the house barn. It was the largest of four barns and the one that housed the horses that were used daily.

Here also, sly laying hens provided the home with eggs. The wily hens tried every trick to secure their eggs for future hatching, but Wind Walker, accompanied by his old, cur dog Reno could ferret out the most carefully camouflaged nest.

"Probably ain't et all day," Walter guessed. He instantly began preparing a supper tray that he could carry to the mansion for the old man's evening meal. He fried up a cottontail rabbit that ranch hand Bobby Baxter had shot that morning.

"How different the cottontail is from them damned old jackrabbits," Walter said aloud to no one. It was true. The meat of the long-eared jack was tough and stringy and was to be only used in cases of starvation and dog food.

The cottontail on the other hand, when prepared correctly, was a succulent bundle of sweet-flavored flesh that was among the finest of dining dishes. Walter Beasley was a highly accomplished rabbit chef. Half the size of the rangy jackrabbit, those who hunted prairie game accounted the fine flavor of the cottontail due to the bunny's feeding on sweet red and white clover.

When the dressed and cleaned rabbit was dipped in a beaten egg and rolled in flour seasoned with salt and black pepper, the morsel was ready to be fried up in a cast iron Dutch oven in good, silver leaf hog lard, flavored with a little saved up bacon drippings. Walter's mouth was watering as he had imagined the meal he would prepare.

It would be an extra meal. The drovers and ranch hands that Walter fed twice daily had their antelope chili, biscuits and stewed apples awaiting them. Breakfast was bacon, biscuits and Arbuckle's chicory. Walter often looked for opportunities to do something special for Old Robert.

When Walter had decided the rabbit was browned well enough and encrusted, he placed the choice backstrap on one of the tin trail plates and lathered it with a deep brown pan gravy. With side dishes of vinegary dandelion greens and a wedge of persimmon pudding, he hurried up to the big house with his offering.

Walter was met on the porch by Juan Garcia who took the plate, peeked beneath the white napkin covering, examined its contents and inhaled the fragrance.

"*Conejo?*" he asked.

"Yeah…It's a cottontail, too. No jackrabbit. Just the best," Walter answered. Garcia disappeared into the house with the food in hand. Walter had thought Juan would have been delighted to see such a fine supper for his old friend. But Walter sensed Juan Garcia was disturbed.

Though late September, Pamela Trav went about tending her flowerbeds as though they had long lives yet ahead. She loved her flowers and selected herbs, but for the last few days her heart was just not in it. Her father-in-law's recent behavior had her disturbed. She was not the only one.

"Pammy, have you seen anything unusual lately 'bout Old Robert?" The inquiry came from her husband, Colin. "He's had me worried a little bit. Just been actin' all strange. He didn't worry 'bout Justin, neither, an' he's 'most healed now."

"Well…I think he's drinking more whiskey than I ever saw before," Pam offered.

Colin countered, "He's always liked to taste…Sip a little. Seems now, though, he's drinkin', not just tasting.

Never knew him to do that. And as far as him spending a whole afternoon in a place like the Staghorn...'Specially the condition it's been in with Burton Cole and Winton Pollard runnin' it into the ground. Well that just ain't him."

"I know, Collie. In the past he wouldn't give those saloon loafers the time of day. Now he's down to the Staghorn two, three days a week. Tell you true, Col, you ought to ask Juan about it. You know, there's nobody knows your stepdaddy better."

Colin knew this to be true. The story of the mysterious friendship between the once poor Scottish immigrant—now a cattle king—with the most famous bandido of the Rio Grande valley was the best-known legend on the Canadian River.

"Walter has made you a special dinner, *Patron*." Garcia was careful with the dish of rabbit. "Conejo," Garcia said.

"What, another damned old jack?" Robert asked.

"Cottontail. Your favorite. Walter cares a great lot about you. You are to him...*Mucho hombre*."

"Well, it's true he's a friend. A good one, too." Robert busied himself with the delicious rabbit backstrap.

"Patron," Garcia began. "I would like to talk to you about something *privado*. Just private for me and you."

"Go ahead, Johnny. We been talking...for what... near 'most forty years?"

"Si. Nearly forty good years. Maybe more. I have trouble now talking with you...It is that you are not the man you have been for so many years."

Robert set aside the plate of food and looked at Juan Garcia.

"How so, Juan?"

"I remember you have liked whisky. You would drink two fingers of Abraham Primble's Caney Creek once or twice a week. You would take little sips and two fingers could last two, three hours at the time you went for your bed. I remember you had no time to spend with lazy men. Men who idled and dallied. Now you drink whiskey from *grande la taza*. You can stay all day in a tavern.

"I see a new man. Not the man I have known for nearly a lifetime. I see a new man who is not so good. How has it come to this? Where did this new *hombre* come from? I remember the Robert who bossed fifty wranglers—drove three thousand cattle to the Dodge railhead. Five months on the trail. Now you need someone to drive your buggy! I am troubled with what I see—All cowboys on the Spur. They are troubled too. Can you talk to me, Patron? Can you tell me what is this change?"

Robert Trav pushed away his rabbit supper. He leaned back into his rocker and stared into the empty fireplace. The room was silent for a long time. It was as if each man knew that the next bit of conversation would be vital. Too important to simply speak without the counsel of thinking first.

"Dang it all to hell, Johnny," Robert managed. "Old Doc is just full of distressin' news these days. He says I got me a problem."

"Problem? *Que pasa?*"

"Says the ticker ain't tickin' just like it ought to. He says I might ought to put my affairs in order. I says to him I ain't got no affairs. He says, 'We all know you're rich. I 'spect you got more than old King Midas. You might be leavin' it someday. Maybe you ought to leave a note or somethin' tellin' us what's buryin' you what to do with yer fortune.'

"I tell him I don't know no King Midas and I don't know how much money I got. May not have any. If there is some somewhere abouts, and if I ain't here no more, we got some smart fellers out to the ranch. We got you, Garcia, and my son, Colin. Colin, why he's got a wife smarter'n him. Pamela, she's quick as a cat. My Pammy...She's the smart one. Any loose money about, she'll give it a good shake."

"So, Doc...He thinks you pretty sick." Garcia was treading lightly.

"Sick! Hell no! Not sick. That old goat thinks I'm a dyin'!'"

"All this drinkin' is 'cause you worried 'bout dyin'?'"

"Worried!? Hell no, I ain't worried about dyin'. For Christ's sake, Johnny, you and me been in enough scrapes, you of all people know I ain't afraid to die. Hoot Mon!" Robert sipped into his old Scottish phraseology. "Everything dies. When God wants me, I'm ready."

"I thought that," said Garcia. "What's about all this drinkin' and layin' around these *podrido hombres* then?"

"I ain't got no fear about dyin'. It's just I ain't ready yet."

"*Madre de Dios!*" Garcia exclaimed. "You think Lord Jesus waits around till you decide you're ready?"

"Just hear me out, Juan. I can die alright. It's just before I do that, I want a little trip."

"A trip, Patron? Where would you go? You've not been five miles from the Spur in thirty years."

"Have too. Went to Seymore, Indiana to fetch that Studebaker buggy."

"Si, si. That is true. So where is it you want to go?"

"Back where it all started. The Rocky Mountains. I want to see it again. I was a trapper there for four years one time. Had me a Indian family. Lived with the Crow, I did. I've got to see it again."

"Caramba! She's no little trip as you call it."

"I had me a woman one time, Juan. Iron Woman she was called. Had us a good life. Till I up and left it. I always meant to go back. Just got caught up in life and never did."

"If it's a woman you need, let's go to Mexico. We can be there in three or four days, and we can find you a señorita to curl the hair of your face. Two señoritas—maybe ten!"

"It's not a woman I want you damned old bandit—Sure as hell not ten! I want to see where it all took place. I want to see bighorn sheep again. There's a high stone cliff there where the water falls from fifty feet. Water got some powerful force. Beaver bigger'n black bears dam up that water, makin' the biggest pond in all Montana. Ain't but a few men ever seen that pond. I saw it with a Crow dog soldier named Bloody Shirt. I want to catch a cutthroat trout in the Yellowstone, Juan. I'd like a roasted cutlet from a Rocky Mountain bighorn. I'd love to see a mountain buffalo again."

"We got buffalo in Texas," Garcia offered. "How many would you like to see?"

"Rocky Mountain buffalo all different Johnny. Got wings, they do. They follow the grass line clean up to the snow cap in the spring. I'd like to see a Crow warrior on his fightin' horse. I'd like to speak the Crow talk again. See myself a real Indian again, Sioux, Cheyenne. A war bonnet red skin."

"How about if I get old Wind Walker to come up to the house and you can talk to him a while?"

"Wind Walker! That old drunk. Why, a wild Indian would scare that old fake to death—Just leave me, Johnny. I've already talked enough. I'm tired out. Still a little drunk too, I guess. Just go on, Juan. I can't talk no more."

Garcia slipped away from his old friend's side as quietly as he was able. When he reached the door, he took one more glance in Old Robert Trav's direction. The old man was staring at the vacant fireplace. *He looks like he's at peace with the world*, Garcia thought. *Mi compadre will sleep soon. I hope he finishes his rabbit.*

Randall, Doctor Rueben Pritchard's brother, took another sip of the raw plain's whiskey. When the burn had subsided enough for him to speak, he hoarsely chided his brother.

"Holy Christ, Reuben. Where in the hell do you buy your whiskey? That's purely panther piss."

"Glad you like it, Randall. It ain't for children. Get you a nose full of that, you know you been somewheres. I prescribe it all the time. For chills and fevers alike. By the third or fourth swallow it smoothens right out. You can kick a catamount's ass if you so inclined."

"Cain't you afford no better?"

"Oh, I can buy higher priced—I just can't find no better."

"You serve somebody a shot of that in Abilene and Marshall Hickock would've hanged your ass."

"Old Wild Bill drunk it himself," Reuben shot back. "That's what made him so wild," he joked.

"I heard it was what killed him back in '76. Enough about whiskey though, Reuben. What about that land parcel? What have you found out about it? I wrote that old Scotsman a letter, but never heard no more about it. I'd like to get it bought and get started settin' up a bank. I got the investors all foamin' at the mouth and cain't get this old bastard to even answer my letter."

"I ain't too sure Old Robert even reads his mail, Randall. No one sees much of him. Stays out on the Spur most all the time. Might be that we can catch his top hand, Garcia, and get a meeting with Trav through him. He comes to town about every Saturday."

"I'm not wasting my time talking to some pepper belly." Randall's expression was one of disgust.

"He might be a pepper belly alright, but he's boss dog over the Broken Spur. During round up, that's more than fifty cowhands."

Randall was angering now. "You can't tell me these hard-assed Texas drovers take orders from a Mexican! I'd say they'd rather whip his ass or maybe shoot him."

Reuben thought a while, then responded, "Well, he's kind of a hard man. Whuppin' his ass wouldn't be all that easy. I'd say grabbin' him would be one helluva mistake. That is unless you knew what you were goin' to do with him. These Spur riders, though, well, seems like they like him. They respect him. I think they'd ride through hell for him. I can't really explain it better'n that. Men just seem to take to him. They seem to like ridin', working with him. And he is a top hand. There's nothing on a horse he can't do. Like I say, the men who work for him think he's just the best. Tell you the truth, Randy, I like him myself. Like I say, he's a top hand."

"Top hand, my ass!" Randall spit. "Damned peasant Mex. Wouldn't take long for me to put him in his place."

"You know, Randall—Juan Garcia's nearly in his eighties I'd guess. I have ten bucks I'd be willing to bet that on your best day he could still kick the living shit out of you."

"You'd bet that ten on a damned Mexican against me, huh? I tell you right up front that's a damned poor bet."

"Let's make it a hundred."

CHAPTER EIGHT
September 1888

Pamela Trav's morning was not going along as well as usual. It was the same old story with the men of Broken Spur. When a problem demanded action or seemed to be somewhat dangerous, there was always more than one man willing to take up the challenge.

The breaking of an outlaw saddle bronc or the roping and dehorning of a wild, range bull would bring volunteers by the score from the ranch hands of the Spur. Even Juan Garcia, now at seventy-seven years old, was no more intimidated by a bucking bronco than he would have been by one of the tabby cats kept in the grain barn for mouse control. This was not the case, however, when the task at hand was one of mundane, boring and very detailed demands. These fell to Pamela.

It was not that she minded being saddled with these onuses, except for the fact that some could be quite demanding of her time, keeping her away from her be-loved horses.

She despised sending Little Buck or Colin to check the hay racks or the watering troughs that served her small, select herd of quarter horse breeding mares. There was Ruby, the sorrel, one of her favorites. Lizzie, the coaly bay, as intelligent as she was beautiful. And then there was Miss

Whiskey, named for her amber color and her flaxen mane and tail. Moving stud horses from the racetracks of Kentucky to the plains of Texas had been a demanding ordeal. Overall, it taken over a year on the trail and the life of her husband, Alex Carstin, killed by determined thieves bent on taking the breeding stock.

Pamela felt that if she had not been rescued by Colin Trav, most certainly her bones would be lying out on the plain somewhere and the blooded stallions would be pulling a settler's plow or buffalo hunting with some Kiowa brave.

This second crop of foaling mares was the culmination of ten years of careful planning and diligent efforts. She wanted to care for them herself. It was, however, difficult to complain about book work and ledger balances. She was, after all, the one who had introduced the record keeping and pedigree tracking system to the cattle and horse operations of the Spur.

When the Spur was operated by Old Robert and Juan Garcia, no one had the faintest idea of how many cattle or horses were on Spur land, let alone the ratio of cows and heifers to bulls or stallions to mares. It all boiled over one morning when she and Colin were having a morning ride around some of the Spur's pastures.

"Look, Colin," she observed. "There're sixteen young bulls in that herd. Only thirty or forty cows, I'd guess, and I don't see any heifers at all."

"Yeah, I suppose that's right. You are a good counter; we'll use you next round up to fetch the tally."

"I don't understand. How would you let that ever happen?" Pamela was perplexed. Now, Colin was baffled.

"What are you gettin' at, Pammy? What's wrong?"

"Lots," she began. "The proper herd mix is one good bull to twenty-five cows. And that pasture's too thin. Good herdsmen back in Illinois try to run eleven head on twenty acres. What with our climate here a bit drier, I'd say we'd do better with ten. Nine maybe. Another thing, there are some pretty young bulls in that group. Why haven't they been castrated and put on grass with a little hay? Every bull on the Broken Spur can't be a breeder. Some are supposed to be beef. That's what a cattle operation is about. Beef!"

"Holy Joe!" Colin exclaimed. "Where did you ever learn so much about cattle?" Colin was somewhat disturbed to hear this remarkable woman speak of such subjects as castration and bull and cow breeding ratios. This was man talk and to hear her speak of the sexual nature of cows and bulls aloud made him uncomfortable.

"It's true my daddy ran a hardware store, but our customers were farmers. I was with them every day," Pamela retorted. "Mostly I listened to their stories about horses, but Illinois and Indiana—They're big cattle states. They don't have cow herds. They don't raise cattle. They feed them! Turn range cattle into prime eating beef. True, they don't have thousands of acres like here. What they do have is corn. Acreage does not make good beef. Corn is the magic. Fill these rangy old Texas cows with enough corn and you'll get a steak that'll melt right in your mouth."

"They don't do things like here in Texas," she continued, "but they do well even with the limited land they have. Big farm in Illinois is about fifty acres, maybe a few have a hundred acres. Not like here in Texas where you've got so much land you don't even use it all. Don't even know how much you have. Small land holders have to work smart."

"Sounds to me like it's time we smartened up too."

Two days later Colin told a stunned, befuddled Juan Garcia that Pamela was to be the new herd boss. Garcia was to make sure all hands gave her the help and respect that she needed.

It took Pamela a month to organize her paperwork and start her new record books. But, when she was finished, she knew where every head was pastured, what bulls were with what cows, and how many heifers were of breeding age and ready to be introduced to those select pastures where carefully evaluated herd bulls awaited. Animal husbandry had come at last to the Broken Spur.

Now though, Juan Garcia had handed her a very different challenge. She was to make the travel arrangements, see to the ticket details and generally supervise Old Robert's upcoming excursion north to the railhead in Kansas and the western trek to the Rocky Mountains.

"Momma, how long does it take to have a baby horse?" Little Buck wanted to know. He looked up at Pamela with his small boy's open and honest face. She loved watching her son. He had Colin's dark hair, but he had her clear blue eyes. At times she thought she could see some of Old Robert in him, too. But that she knew was impossible, as Colin had been rescued from Comancheros as a child by Robert and Juan Garcia. Colin was Robert's stepson.

"Why do you ask?" Pamela answered. She felt her son at ten was a little young to be told about the breeding procedures of livestock.

"Mister Garcia says Junebug's gonna have a baby horse. I want to play with it when it comes. Where's it come from anyhow, Momma?"

"Well, right now it's in Junebug's tummy. When it's ready, it'll come out and you can play with it then."

"Does it hurt? When it comes out of her tummy? Is Junebug gonna be okay? I don't want nothin' to hurt her."

"Well, I guess it hurts a little, but she will love that foal so much she won't pay any attention to the hurt at all.'

"Foal? What's a foal?" Little Buck was filled with questions.

"That's the right name for a baby horse." Pamela explained. "When they get a little bigger, we call them colts if they're boys or fillies if they're girls. Then when they are about two years old, we call them horses."

"Well, how long is it gonna take?"

"You know, that's a good question. See, horses are a little different than some animals. Now, if a momma hog is going to have some little pigs, it will take three weeks and three months and three days. When your dog Susie had those puppies last year, it took her sixty-three days.

"But horses are different. We can never be sure just exactly how long it's going to be. Some mares will give birth at eleven months. Some mares may take as long as thirteen months, and I've heard of even fourteen. So, because we can never be exactly sure, we just say it takes about a year."

"Do I have to wait a year for Junebug's baby—I mean foal—then?"

"It won't be that long. Junebug will have that baby horse before you know it."

"You said baby horse, Momma. It's a foal!" Pamela handed him a gingersnap. "Kin I have another for Junebug, Momma? You know what, Momma? Junebug and I play games sometimes."

"Oh? What kind of games can you play with a horse?" Little Buck chewed the gingersnap noisily.

"Well, you know when she puts her ears out front, I know she's askin' me a question. You know? Like what time is it? Or when are we gonna eat? I tell her and then kiss her on the nose and then we just both laugh. We laugh right out loud, Momma." Without another word the boy skipped out the back door and across the yard to the corral with Junebug's cookie.

"You go play now," she called to the retreating youngster. "Momma's busy planning Grandpa Robert's trip." She watched him skip away.

God, I am so lucky! she thought. Pamela, then assumed the concerned countenance that all mothers do when they learn their child has an imaginary playmate. Sometimes, she knew it might be another child. A giant maybe. When she was a girl Pamela had a princess for a friend.

"My boy has a horse for a playmate," she thought aloud. "One that can laugh."

CHAPTER NINE

Red Stick crawled the last few yards on his belly. Hidden in the folds of grama grass, he had reached the south edge of the Canadian River. With the battered army field glasses, he began his daily vigil of spying on the home-site of the Broken Spur.

An old, retired cavalry trooper was living in a little shack above one of the run-offs of the river. Red Stick had killed him in his sleep one night for his boots. The handmade footwear of the Comanche could never com-pare with United States Cavalry boots for wear in this wild country.

He could not understand how his Comanche brethren had allowed this to happen. His grandfather had told him it began when a white trapper and a Mexican ban-dit had agreed with the old chieftain Buffalo Hump to kill no buffalo north of the Canadian nor south of the Red. This enormous wedge of land located between the two rivers had then, somehow, become the domain of these two interlopers. This Robert. This Garcia.

They had lived in peace with the Comanche and Kiowa for decades by allowing the natives to commandeer a calf or two when the buffalo moved north out of hunt-ing range. They gave each other a wide berth and never associated. The former trapper turned cattleman and his

Mexican friend held the land in a form of mutual, absentee goodwill. However, they were never seen unarmed.

"*Squahalla.*" Red Stick spat the Comanche word for ridiculous. This was some of the finest land anywhere in the vast area the white men had called Texas. Not only rich in fresh water, buffalo, deer, and antelope, but the size of the area also bounded by the two rivers was overwhelming. To concede such a rich parcel to two drifters was, to Red Stick, extremely poor governing on the part of the old chieftains.

He longed for the days when he had followed Peta Nicone and his son, Quanah Parker. These were great warrior chieftains before the time of the Palo Duro Canyon event. He could not help a chuckle escaping his lips. He always laughed when he thought of the name Quanah. A Comanche word for "he who smells sweet."

Red Stick had to admit he had never noticed how Quanah Parker may have smelled, but he knew him as a fearless warrior. Cunning and cruel. Dedicated to death for white pilgrims. The more terrible the death he could inflict, the more terror he could plant among the settlers. Red Stick loved the ways of war and the spreading of terror by savage torture and brutal wasting.

He and a select group of the Quahadi clan, along with Comanche aristocracy White Knife, Horseback, Milky Way and Wild Horse, ravaged the land west to Arizona territory, south to the Rio Grande, and even into Mexico. Constantly pursued by Captain Ranald Mackenzie's U.S. Cavalry troopers along with Texas Rangers, these marauders still held sway over Oklahoma, Texas, and parts of Mexico for more than a dozen years.

In 1874, the Quahadi were joined by a group of Kiowa, Cheyenne, and Arapaho warriors led by Poor Buffalo and Lone Wolf, to wage a concerted effort to defeat Mackenzie. These were the finest days of the Comanche Nation prior to the great horse massacre of the Palo Duro Canyon.

"His men all hate him, President Grant. They say his discipline is too tough, but he's one hard fighting son of a bitch. You'd have a hard time finding a better man holding the reins."

William Worth Belnap was a decorated soldier, but he found it difficult not to think as his previous civilian calling. He was a lawyer. Always would be. Once the Government Administrator to the territory of Iowa, he was now the nation's thirtieth Secretary of War, serving Ulysses S. Grant. The presidency of Ulysses Grant had begun March 4th, 1869, after another of his hard-fought battles. This time instead of fervent southern rebels it was with the dedicated Democrats and their candidate, Horatio Seymour.

Seymour's popularity was unquestionable. Twice the governor of New York, and an avid enemy of slavery, he posed a threat to any candidate. Even a great war hero.

"If he had never touched on that stupidity of prohibiting the making of whiskey, he would have been even more formidable," Grant allowed. "Americans are going to make their whiskey no matter what. I, for one, am damned glad they do!"

No one had believed the nation could support a three-party system. Actually, the once respected Whig party only existed as extended members of the Democrats, as they were absorbed into the democratic party in 1856. That same year Lawrence, Kansas, was burned to the ground by pro-slavers.

This heartless and ruthless act would serve as a prelude to the American Civil War. The absorption of the oldest American political party was a fact most voters found hard to believe. Some of their revered founding fathers were indeed Whigs.

Both Whigs and Democrats, now joined together, were firmly secure in the governing of the nation and believed no one could overcome them in a free election. Abraham Lincoln, though, had elected to run for President as a candidate of the newly formed Republican party. He had endeared himself to the nation with such a strong bonding that his party would someday become the "Grand Old Party." The GOP.

As for Grant, first there was the Civil War. Next came politics and the election. Now, late into Grant's term in office, he found himself facing yet another adversary.

"I'm sick of hearing the word Comanche," Grant retorted. "For God's sake, we've made peace with and relocated every other band of Indians in all of Texas and Lord knows that's a plenty. We've been fighting these bastards since the Mexican war back in 1840. What's it going to take to get rid of them? Why don't the troopers just blow 'em to hell? For Christ's sake, we have cannon firepower. Why not just blow them away?"

Belnap had a ready answer.

"If the Comanche would stand and fight, that's exactly what would happen. But, it's not their way. They set up an ambush, shoot four or five troopers, and run for that high grass country. It's the horses too, Mister President. Believe it or not, they've got a better light cavalry than we have. Every one of them has four of five horses stashed along their getaway. They can refresh half a dozen times a day. Once they get into the staked plains, they can just wear our troopers out. A sea of grass. Without a tree or a stone to take a reckoning by. They just disappear. Set up a new ambuscade. That area is so immense. No landmarks. Just like the oceans. Grass as far as the eyes can see."

"Just how big is that area anyway?" the President wanted to know.

"Our cartographers and surveyors say 250 miles long by 200 miles wide. Maybe 50,000 square miles."

"Damn! That's the size of New England."

"Bigger," Belnap said.

"And you think Ranald Mackenzie is the right man, do you? I do know some things about him. Top of his class at West Point. Gettysburg, Roundtop, Appomattox—hardly missed a single major battle. A fighter alright. I'll give you that. Matter of fact he seems to attract bullets. Every big fight he seems to get shot. Wounded six times, I think. Every wound led to a promotion. Hell, I made him a brigadier. Next thing I know Lincoln makes him a Major General. I'm starting to think that sumbitch gonna pretty soon have my job—O'course, I'm just pokin' fun."

"But his ambitions do beg the question," the President went on. "I'm just wondering if he might not cause more trouble than we have already. He's called Bad Hand you know. Got a few fingers shot off. They tell me when a Comanche sees a battle scar like that it's almost like a religion to them."

"Every commander that has ever sided with him says he's the best soldier they've ever seen." Belnap continued. "Besides that, on another subject if you will. We talk about the trouble we already have. This newspaper man—this John O'Sullivan. He's a bigger problem than a few hostiles. He never lets up with his constant preaching about this so-called Manifest Destiny. He has the public up in arms. Everywhere you go he's already been there. He has the public believing it's a mission commanded by God to kill the red man and take the land from 'sea to shining sea,' as he puts it. Hasn't been a man with such hate for Indians since Andy Jackson moved the Creeks and Cherokees to the Oklahoma territory. Whigs and Democrats, too. Right along with him. Kill the Indians off like vermin. He's got them saying that it's God's plan."

"Same bullshit they put out back in 1840 about a few Spanish missions in California." Grant allowed. "What did they accomplish? Got us a war with Mexico is what they did." The President halted his oratory and took a deep breath. "But, all in all, I guess we've got no choice. Turn your war dog Mackenzie loose. Maybe God will forgive us sometime. 'Specially if the Comanche roast his ass over a slow fire."

CHAPTER TEN

Pamela finally determined that arranging a travel itinerary in the wild country of Texas was far different from the same chore in Chicago. The problem ten years past was simply not enough railroads. Now in 1888, there were too many, with spur tracks springing up everywhere bringing about a great deal of confusion. Some were unfinished. Some went nowhere and others seemed to have no beginning or end.

The financial success of the Southern Pacific and the Union Pacific had attracted hordes of would-be entrepreneurs willing to invest in railroads and unscrupulous contractors and builders welcomed their funds. A common practice was to open an office advertising a new railhead to be established in some desirable location, accept investors' funds, then lay down a few miles of track, take those funds and disappear forever.

A mishmash of these deserted tracks caused mass confusion to travelers anywhere west of Saint Louis. Fortunately, Pamela learned there was a reliable spur running north from the Texas panhandle to Dodge City, Kansas. This had been strategically constructed to accommodate the Texas herds moving north to transportation east by rail to the meat packing empire of Chicago by adjoining the Union Pacific.

Through the writing of a dozen or more letters, Pamela learned that Old Robert could journey to Dodge City by rail using this spur. From there she was assured there was available rail transport to Denver. How Robert would get from Denver across Wyoming territory and into Montana was still a mystery.

"You've done enough," Garcia told her. "Once we get to Denver, I'm certain there will be someone who can give us the directions to Montana. Those towns north of here aren't as out-of-the-way as we are. I'm not worried. We'll find the way."

Walter drove the two old men—in their new suits, hats and boots—far out into the prairie where they had been told a train stop was located. When they reached the spot the station was to be, there was nothing. Just a passenger car setting alone on a stretch track that ran north.

The south end of the car was fenced by cross ties piled as high as the observation blind. The three sat in the buggy completely confused. Just when they were about to wheel the Studebaker about, a hatless young man in bib overalls got down from the train car and approached them.

"Ya'll agoin' to Dodge, are ye?"

"Thought we might," Walter answered.

"Jest go ahead and stuff your gear in that there car and make yourself comfortable. Sometime today or maybe tomorrow a engine'll come along and hook us up. We'll make Dodge in a day or two. Might be three. They's more cars to hook up with along the way. But, don't you worry none. We gonna be jest fine."

It worked pretty much as the young man had said. Walter had carried most of the luggage and two rifles aboard. Then he wished the pair well and mounted the buggy, clucked to the team and started the trip back to Broken Spur.

Both Robert and Garcia were sound asleep on the hard wooden seats of the car when there was a resounding loud crash, accompanied by a bone-jarring jolt, nearly dislodging them from their seats. Only a few moments later, a shrill whistle assaulted the travelers' ears, there was another unsettling jolt as the train moved forward and, at last, they were on their way.

It was midmorning before the train stopped again, this time to add two more cars to the chain. While stopped, a short, heavy woman boarded the train car holding a large, wicker basket of food for sale. She had broad slabs of head cheese sandwiched with thick brown bread slices and small glass bottles of warm beer sealed with cork. Garcia and Robert agreed the molasses cookies were her best offering.

As the train headed out, Robert and Garcia sat facing each other enjoying the food, but mostly reliving the days they had shared in the past. They gazed out the window at the lands they were rolling through and loving every minute of it. Neither had ridden a train before, but each swore this would not be the last time. This enjoyment lasted all the way to Dodge City. In Dodge, as Garcia had predicted, they had no trouble locating a northbound train to Denver. The two compadres continued to enjoy each hour they were together. It would be in Denver that misfortune struck.

CHAPTER ELEVEN

Red Stick couldn't understand yet why he was so alone in his mission. Comanches had hated the intrusion of white settlers since the 1830s, and now, after the 1874 battle of Palo Duro Canyon, they accepted their defeat and allowed the whites to tell them where and how they were to live.

He could no more understand their acceptance of defeat than he could explain the vastness of the *Llano Escatado*. The whites called it the staked plains, but the Comanche and the Mexicans still held to the name the Spanish explorer, Francisco Vasquez Coronado, had given it three hundred years before. Llano Escatado.

"One cannot navigate here," Coronado had declared. "A vast sea of grass with not a single tree or bush or stone in sight. An ocean of gently waving grass with only the arc of the sun and the placement of the stars to give direction." And then the question: direction to where? Was this infinite plain to go on forever? And if it did end, what was at the culmination?

True, many small lakes and ponds called potholes or sinks were scattered about within the immense square miles, but it was also true that there were vast stretches without a single drop of moisture. If a traveler did not know how to locate these tiny oases, a terrible death awaited them. These depressions in the earth were below the tall grass line, so that one might pass within a few yards of life-giving water and never know it was there.

Red Stick knew where they were. At least, some of them. He had traveled here as a boy with his father, Enzo Antaya, a former French fur trapper who knew about grasslands, horses, cattle, and buffalo, and had loved Red Stick's mother, Birdsong, until she had died.

"Father, why is my name so different from all the other Quahadi?" Red Stick asked often.

"It is because *you* are different. You are half white. My son. My fine son. You are named for a place."

"Is it a good place, Father?"

"A wonderful place. A place of laughter and music. Pretty people too."

"Were you in this place, Father?"

"For a while." His father always became still when he told this.

"Why would you leave such a place, Father? Could we go there sometime?" This was always when his father searched for another subject to speak of.

"In spring and fall, Baton Rouge." His father used the French words for Red Stick when he spoke to his son. "Watch for the ducks and wild geese. When you see them set down or rise up from the grass, there will be the water. They come here in the spring to lay the eggs and raise the young. In the fall they leave. No one knows where they go, but they fly away to the south."

"Mark well what you see here in the spring and fall. In the summer you can catch the wild cayuse at those watering places, and in winter you can kill buffalo. Buffalo must journey south from Colorado snow in the winter, and they come here to the banks of the Canadian River. Wild cattle can be caught here, too."

These instructions had served him well, especially now that he had become unwelcome among his Comanche brethren.

"We have lost all," Elk Hunter had said to him. "Without our horses we can make no more war. You are lobo. You cause many troubles. We will live now in peace. The horses lay dead in Palo Duro. We can make no more war."

"I can steal horses! You can steal horses, too. We must not give up the land to the white men," Red Stick raged.

"Go from us. You are no longer one of us. You bring much trouble. You are lobo."

Ranald Mackenzie hated the Quahadi more than any of the enemy he had met in the War Between the States. The Confederates would stand and fight to the last man. These Comanche, however, were constantly sniping at his command and then disappearing before he could return the strike. Four of his troopers, all good personal friends, had lost their lives to these hidden riflemen and archers. Finally, his scouts had discovered the main tribal camp on the plains at the mouth of the Palo Duro Canyon just north of the Canadian River.

His command launched such an unsuspected and ferocious charge that the warriors were forced to flee on foot, leaving their horse herd behind. Then Mackenzie's troops commandeered the horse herd and trapped them within the canyon.

With the horses secured, Mackenzie set his soldiers to burning everything the Comanche had left behind. Considering how they had been forced to bolt without warning, this amounted to all that they owned. Tepees, robes, weapons, bedding—everything.

He then put his men to work destroying the horses. More than two thousand head were shot by his riflemen at the rate of two per minute, one hundred and twenty-five head per hour. The surviving Quahadi lined the cliffs above the canyon and watched as every horse was put to death. The dead beasts were left to rot, and for days the stench poisoned the air of the canyon and broke the hearts and the spirits of the boldest tribe Texas had ever known.

Dejected, horseless, and homeless, they walked to the land reserved for them. Without the horses the Comanche nation was gone forever. Except for a few who would never surrender. They were the lobos. The zorros. Red Stick was one of these. They vowed to fight forever.

"Sheriff Arnette! You'd better come quick. Uncle Ike Pauley's coming up Pamela Street with his old flat wagon. Somethin's terrible wrong!"

No one remembered ever seeing Winton Pollard this excited. Generally, he lolled about in front of the jail sharpening his pocketknife and socializing with the passersby. Occasionally, he stocked the grocery shelves in Gurske's for fifty cents a day. When he had an extra two bits, he'd have a shot and a beer in the Staghorn.

Winton was well known as a beer nurse who could make a short stein last about three hours. Drinking his beer this way, he could kibitz with Lisa Strong, the house poker player, while she waited for a game, or jawbone with bartender Fred about his past daring adventures. To see him in this highly agitated state, Arnette thought was unusual to say the least.

"Matter?" Tom Arnette asked. "What're you talking about, Winton? What's wrong?"

"Come see. Old Uncle Ike's got a real mess on his hands. Just terrible—just terrible."

Stepping out on the boardwalk in front of his office, Arnette saw the old man and his decrepit wagon drawn along by an old and work-worn mule. Seven or eight of the Travis townsfolk walked along the wagon side. Arnette could see a few of the women were weeping. He stepped off the walkway and into the street. Closer now, he could see there was something being carried in the wagon with a tarpaulin covering it.

"Whatcha got there, Uncle Ike?" the sheriff queried.

"Come see, Tom." The old man stopped his mule and stepped down from his wagon seat. Walking to the side of the wagon, he drew back the tarp. The little crowd let out a gasp of horror. Arnette felt an uncontrollable rise of bile in his throat.

Three charred corpses lay side by side on the wagon's floor, faces burned beyond recognition. Relentless and intense heat had caused the bodies to contort into grotesque and unnatural forms. Bluebottle flies aggravated the pitiful remains.

"My God, Uncle Ike. What is this? Who in the world are these poor people?"

"Well, you can see it's pretty hard to tell for sure. But what I think is these here are the remains of the

Prescott family, Edmond and his wife, Paula. Little feller there is their boy. Junie, I think they called him. I'se over by there this morning and stopped in to say how-do. Found this here mess, I did. Place burned to the ground. House, barn and all. Whoever did all this kilt their milk cow. Family dog too."

"Good Lord! Who'd kill a milk cow? A dog?" Arnette was baffled by the needless destruction.

"Old time Comanche way, Tom. Kill everything, burn the rest. Edmond, he had hisself four brood mares and a big stud horse too. Big bay brute he was. Loved them mares. Kept after 'em all the time, in season or not. 'Course no Comanche'd ever kill a horse. Anyhow, horses—all gone. Stole, I reckon. Guns, too. Edmond used to be a Ranger, you know. A captain, I think he was. Had more'n a dozen guns. Rifles and such. They's gone, too. Looks to me like old-time Comanche works."

"That don't seem likely," Arnette allowed. Comanche been on the reservations five, maybe six years now."

"Mebbe so. Anyways, I'se around here back when the Comanche was one hell of a problem. Seen a lot of their mischief, I did. Jest look at the heads of these poor folks. All been scalped, don't you see. Mebbe you got a better idea—But I'm thinkin' Comanche, Tom."

The constable of Travis, Texas, barely heard the last words of Uncle Ike Pauley. Tom Arnette had removed his hat and placed his hand on the charred foot of the smallest of the three. Deep in prayer, he was pleading with his Lord Jesus to take this child, restore him and welcome him into the kingdom.

Hernando Ulando had reached the last of his strength. He, a lifelong professional soldier, had no fear of his approaching death. His strong Catholic faith assured him of his awaiting Savior. He had no dread for himself. Rather, he feared for the company of one hundred twenty conquistadors that trailed his doomed reconnaissance detachment.

These, under the command of Francisco Vasquez de Coronado, were on the march from Vera Cruz north and east along the *El Camino Real*, the King's Highway. This royal road was in truth only a primitive trail. However, it was superbly marked by the footfalls of dozens of mounted troops as well as scores of Spanish infantry. They had trod this thoroughfare since Garcia Lopez de Cardenas made his historic trek to the Grand Canyon in 1540.

All who marched and rode here believed this eventually would lead to El Dorado. The city of gold. A shrewd Pawnee captive, El Turco, had promised the Spanish knights that he could and would lead them not only to El Dorado but also to a fabulous metropolis called Quivera. A land of gold and silver

Coronado's Captain Hernando Alvarado allowed the Pawnee to lead their expedition through what would become Texas and Oklahoma territory north into the lands of the Wichita where they found only cornfields and grass huts. No treasure there. Only poverty among one of the first farmer tribes. Realizing he had been lied to, Alvarado had El Turco executed by the garrote, hanged by his heels, and left to rot.

He turned his detachment back onto the El Camino and returned to Mexico City. He was dismayed when he found his valiant leader, Francisco, in the throes of a fatal fever. In 1554 Coronado passed away and, along with him, many of the dreams of El Dorado and Quivera. The Spaniards, hungry for success and riches, turned away from North America to search elsewhere for the glory they craved.

North America truly never lost all of its appeal to these expeditionary forces of King Phillip II and his wife Mary, Queen of England. However, simply by chance, they found a ready treasure trove awaiting them. It was not in the north as they had expected. The more immediate and more attainable wealth lay to the south within the Spanish Lake.

That beautiful sea was named the Caribbean for the fierce Carib Indians who once had lived there and had seemed poised to welcome the Spanish. It was as if they all had been asleep awaiting the kiss of Spain to awaken them. A comparatively gentle sea dotted by some of the most hospitable islands in the New World. These would make Spain the richest kingdom in Europe with its gold and silver from Peru. Yet even gold and silver were paled by the fortunes earned by hundreds of Spanish ships laden with sugar and coffee.

In 1598, Phillip II died. His wife, Mary, Queen of England had died of probable cancer in 1558, ending the very complicated union of these two. Their marriage had more to do with reestablishment of Catholicism in England than with love. Indeed, it is believed that "Bloody Mary" had convicted and executed by the fiery stake more than three hundred heretics.

And so, it would be Phillip III (son of Phillip II by his fourth marriage) who would command the forces in the Caribbean that brought unimaginable wealth to Spain. His plan was a simple one: as the riches came to Spain, he would build more ships, enlist more men, buy more horses and ship all to the Spanish Lake.

The lands to the north—for a while—had lost some of their allure as the Caribbean islands were proving to be the rightful treasury of Spain. But thirty years later, Lieutenant Hernando Ulando found himself in another expeditionary journey onto the north American continent purely as an information gathering effort.

Were there treasures here that previous adventurers had overlooked? The cadre of one hundred twenty under the command of Capitan Ernesto Ortega were charged to reexplore these lands. Even if no treasure could be found, there were still natives to bring to the church.

Vasquez and five of his comrades had been ordered by Capitan Ortego to take the point of the marching column. Their mission was to scout for food and to warn of approaching warring parties of the Kaw.

Stephano Garcia, Vasquez's closest friend, had remarked to Hernando one morning as they topped a rise and gazed at a plain that stretched endlessly below them, "Horses! Look at all those horses! I did not know this land had horses! It's wonderful!"

"Not so wonderful, Stephano. This land had never seen a horse until we of Spain came here. Those are the

children of the horses left behind by the dead conquis-
tadores of our past. Soldiers of Spain. Our grandfathers.
Dead from Indian fights and starvation."

"It cannot be, Hernando! If the soldiers died. If
they starved why not the horses?"

"Horses can live on grass and water. Soldiers cannot. These horses were abandoned by the dying. They have
been feeding and breeding for more than thirty years. Cattle
too. Brought here to serve as food for the armies they are
now as wild as the wind. They were once small bands of
five or six. Now they are dozens. Sometimes there could be
hundreds. These were once the work force of Spain. Now
they are the wild cattle. The wild horse of the Americas."

Hernando recalled his words to Stephano as he lay
failing among the bodies of his five fellows. The ambuscade of the Kaw had come as a total surprise and in only
minutes the forward advance party lay dead or dying. The
last thing that Hernando Vasquez would ever see was the
retreat of the Kaw warriors as they rode away with the six
saddlers and the four pack horses. With his last breath he
called out, "*Caballos—mi caballos!*"

CHAPTER THIRTEEN
Early October 1888

The train had barely stopped at the Denver Depot when Juan Garcia noticed the ashen color of Robert Trav. The two men had enjoyed their time on the train. They had talked and relived their years of adventure together. Completely relaxed, Robert had told Garcia many of the wonderful things about fur trapping the Crow country.

His tales of the people themselves were spellbinding. They were just gathering up their parcels and starting to leave the train when Garcia became aware that something was seriously wrong with his old friend.

"Patron!" he cried. "Are you well? You are so pale."

Robert's mouth was open. There was no sound.

"What's wrong, Rob? Tell me what I can do for you."

Robert's answer was to clutch at his chest, collapse between the seats and fall to the floor of the train car.

To Garcia it seemed an endless time, but actually the conductor had both Robert and Garcia in a carriage on the way to a local doctor's office in less than twenty minutes.

Doctor Hugh Greene's office was another twenty minutes away and by now Garcia was himself in a state of shock. This was his oldest friend. His compadre. They had shared good times and hard times. They had stood shoulder to shoulder and faced their enemies together. They had suffered heat and drought, snow and ice. They had killed men who were attempting to take what they were building, and they had killed others who had attempted to bring wrongdoings to the lands of the Spur.

"Some men just ain't fit to live," Robert Trav had declared when faced with these hard choices. All in all, they had risked their lives and their fortunes each one for the other.

Garcia loved this old man, and the thought of losing him was near unbearable.

Once inside Doctor Greene's office, Juan Garcia began to feel somewhat better. Nicely appointed and smelling strongly of some clean-smelling chemicals, the office gave off an aura of professionalism. A pretty nurse in a light blue uniform with a snowy white apron had, with Garcia's help, stretched Robert on an examination table and was bathing his face with cool water.

"Ain't you just the prettiest little thing?" Robert said through a sly smile. Garcia felt better instantly. He thought he could detect a bit of color returning to Robert's face.

"You just mind your manners now, Romeo," she jokingly chided him. "You are just not up to any heavy romancing right now." Garcia could only smile.

Doctor Hugh Greene turned out to be a large man with frosted red hair and a matching, closely cropped beard. He took great pains in examining Robert, covering his upper body completely with his stethoscope. The examination was taking a long time and Garcia was becoming disturbed again.

"Can you tell me something about him?" Juan asked. "His condition? Is he going to be alright?"

"Yeah, I can tell you a few things." The doctor suspended the stethoscope from his neck and took a seat on a bench near Garcia's chair.

"First of all, his heart isn't all it should be. That's pretty normal though for a man of his age. What is he— near eighty, I'd guess?"

"Not sure. Eighty sounds about right. Is this a heart attack?"

Doctor Greene lit a greenish cigar and leaned back against the wall. He took several hearty puffs on the cigar and studied it, carefully rolling it between his pudgy fingers. Looking over the top of his glasses, he studied Garcia. He wondered if a Mexican could understand an American diagnosis.

"It's not a heart attack," he said at last. "At least, not a full blown, low down, go to hell heart attack. It's what we call an angina hit. Kind of a baby heart attack. It's not fatal—more of a warning. Kind of letting you know what's coming."

"Can you make him well?" Garcia was almost pleading.

"No. But, I think I can make him feel better. I can give him something that'll greatly help the angina. Probably help him live longer, feel better. But you need to know it's a treatment. Not a cure."

"Treatment?"

"We can use some nitroglycerin. Make him liven right up."

"Nitroglycerin?" Garcia was aghast.

"Don't get yourself all excited. We been using nitro pills since about 1867. Feller named Lauder Brunton found out about the headaches. In 1876, another English doctor by name of Murell picked up on some work another doctor named Nobel had done a long time ago, and he's the one who came up with this pill that takes angina pains away. Pretty safe stuff. Here's one of the pills."

He held a tiny tablet to show Garcia. Garcia watched as Greene slipped the pill into Robert's mouth. Garcia thought it the smallest pill he had ever seen.

"Just let it dissolve and then swallow it up with as much spit as you can raise." Minutes passed with no one speaking.

Robert finally said, "Damn, sure gives you a headache, don't it?"

"But, how does your chest feel?" The doctor wanted to know.

"Pretty damn good. Matter of fact, just my head's throbbin' a little. I'm doin' alright."

It could be said the little pill made Garcia feel better, too.

"I can't believe it," Garcia said. "Who would have ever thought nitroglycerin could be used for something other than to blow the hell out of things."

"Well, them English doctors, like Doctor Murell," replied Doctor Greene. "See, there's a lot of doctors over there. They got time to go to laboratories and clinics. They can do experiments. They have the time to do those things. Here in America, we don't have so many docs, you know. We're too busy to go experimenting with anything, Especially here on the frontier. I'm busy daylight till dark. I'm always treating a horse bite, maybe a shooting, and knife fights, too. Probably treat five or six cases of the clap every week."

"I know about guns and knives—but what is this clap? I don't think I've heard of that." Garcia slapped his hands together with a decisive smack.

"I'd guess that where you came from they'd say too many señoritas. Or at least, one too many."

"Aye caramba!" Garcia understood. "How do you treat that?"

"I'll not tell you that, except to say it takes a little rubber hose and a small scalpel. It ain't pretty."

Robert remained in the doctor's care for three days. When the two travelers told the doctor they'd like to continue their trip, he was resolute in his advice.

"Go home," he said. "You need to be at home. You need the comfort and dependability of things you are familiar with. I'm sending you a good supply of that nitro. You only take it when you need to. If you need more, drop us a line and we'll send it to you wherever you say. 'Course send us along a little money too."

"How much?" Garcia asked.

"A double eagle ought to buy enough for a year. Depends on how often you need it. I got Nurse Withrow fixing you some laudanum, if you really get to hurtin'."

"Does laudanum stop pain?" Robert queried.

"No. Pain's still there. Tricks your brain into thinking the pain's gone. Makes you loco too. You get to hurting bad enough you need the laudanum, you need to get to a doctor right away."

"Our doc's a pretty far piece from our ranch house. You reckon I'll be alright to ride? Buggy, maybe?"

"If you feel bad enough to put up with the taste of that skunk bile, you get your skinny ass in bed and send your pal, Mexican Joe, here, to bring that doctor to you. You been here three days—give the nurse fifteen dollars on your way out. Sorry about your trip. Better you stay close to home."

A wire was sent to Travis in care of Constable Tom Arnette.

ALERT COOK WALTER AT BROKE SPUR. STOP. MEET TRAIN SUNDAY. STOP. SAME PLACE AS BEFORE. STOP. BRING STUDEBAKER. STOP. GARCIA.

Robert was despondent that he was to miss the opportunity to see the Crow country again.

"Damned old pill-pushing sawbones. Wrecked our trip, Johnny. I tell you the truth, some men just ain't fit to live."

Garcia tolerated his old friend complaining all the way back to Texas. The last of the Rio Grande bandits was just glad that his compadre Robert was alive.

Red Stick's successful raid on the Prescott farm had provided him and his three lobos with the vitally needed horses. He decided a war council was needed next. Far out in the Escatado on the bank of a large pothole, he and his three confederates had set up a cold camp. They had no fire and ate some of the raw bacon taken from the Prescott raid along with some home-canned peaches.

He looked over his trio of warriors carefully. It had taken him over a month to gather them, and they were not much to look at, he had to admit. Gone were the regal appearances of the plains' warrior. The feathered headdresses, buckskins, hair roaches—all gone now.

All lost in the Mackenzie fires at Palo Duro Canyon. Now, dressed in hand-me-down and stolen clothing, the band looked more like vagabonds or railroad hobos than Comanche dog soldiers.

Only four total. Red Stick had ridden with Quanah Parker in a band of two hundred. Once they'd been called the lords of the plains. No more. Still these three were willing fighters, unlike the Comanche who had decided to fight no more and just sit upon the administration's reservation and eat government beef.

First was Grey Wolf. He was the smallest of the three, but probably the best horseman. Preferring bareback riding to save weight on his mount, he could ride like the wind, even jumping over fallen logs, fences and hedges. He was also one of the cruelest torture masters Red Stick had ever encountered. Red Stick thought that Grey Wolf's delight in causing pain and terror could prove very useful.

Buffalo Horn was a tall, thin man. He was the best shot of the three with the rifle and quite good with the bow and arrow as well. Normally stoic and quiet, he hated the whites as much as Red Stick did. Also, like Red Stick, he hated his Comanche brethren who had elected to resign themselves to a reservation. Once he had revered Quanah Parker, but now he despised the old war chief who had taken the white man ways.

One of the Quahadi had found a white man's newspaper and had brought it into camp for all to see. In the well-worn and ragged publication was a photograph of Quanah wearing a black suit with a necktie and a bowler derby. While some tribal members were amused by the image, Buffalo Horn was at once heartbroken and furious.

The fourth of Red Stick's band was the most unlikely of all. Michael was not an Indian at all. Rather, he was a towheaded, blue-eyed young man revered by Red Stick as the most intelligent and cunning of his squad. Taken as a captive in the Red River wars at age five, Michael had become the adopted son of no less than six major warriors of the Quahadi. Carefully nurtured by his half-dozen fathers, he had become skilled in the ways of the hunt and, more importantly, he was a respected dog soldier, a solo fighter and terrorist. When the band of warriors Michael had loved all of his life had given in to the soldier Mackenzie and moved to the government's reserved lands, his disappointment in their courage led him to becoming a lobo like his confederate Red Stick.

Now when Red Stick looked upon the little string of horses they had taken in their last raid, he could feel his heart swell within his chest. These horses were the encouragement that he needed. If one had horses, all things were possible. These were the principal weapons of war.

"We will attack and defeat this place called Broken Spur," Red Stick declared. He cradled Edmond Prescott's model 1873 Winchester lovingly in his arms as he spoke. The eyes of the brigand trio widened. He was proposing a daring mission indeed.

The riders of the Spur were universally accepted to be a hard bunch, dangerous to a man. While Red Stick let his startling statement sink in, he went back to admiring his new rifle.

It was *the* gun of its time. The 44-40 caliber was the most powerful repeating rifle, firing a forty-four caliber bullet backed with forty grains of black gunpowder. Further, from the Prescott raid he had acquired an almost new Colt single action revolver. This beautiful pistol was clad in shiny nickel plate with grips of yellowed ivory. More importantly, it fired the same caliber bullet as the rifle.

For any man who might find himself in need of a gun this was the finest combination of the day, a rifle and handgun with interchangeable cartridges. For all of his life, Red Stick had been plagued with ineffective and obsolete, junk weapons. For an Indian to own a combination such as he had in his possession made him as well-armed as any Texas Ranger.

Buffalo Horn also was handling a new rifle. Well, at least new to him. A Civil War Spencer carbine was not as fine as a new Winchester, but nonetheless, was a very effective repeating rifle. It could fire seven fifty-caliber bullets as fast as a man could operate the lever. Short and light it was indeed a fine weapon for a man on a horse. He also had one of Prescott's pistols. The heavy Remington 45 was a powerful sidearm and an effective war club.

"How can we fight the Spur riders?" Buffalo Horn wanted to know. "They have many horses. Many guns. They are men of great courage."

"Squahalla!" Red Stick yelled. "I do not intend to fight them on their terms. We will not fight them boldly. Slyly as the rattler. Quietly as the panther. We will inflict so much pain and hurt, they will die many times."

"How can this be?" It was Grey Wolf. "Men can die once. Only once."

"Michael and me have talked 'bout this," Red Stick said. "Tell them, Michael. Tell them how a man can die every day."

Michael took his time and told his story carefully. He wanted all to see that this was something he had given a great deal of thought to.

"It is true that if we rode into the gates of the Broken Spur as mounted warriors, we would certainly kill two, three, maybe five, before they would shoot us down. If we were to do murder under the cover of night, we could kill two, maybe three. Perhaps, we could escape. But what would happen? The next day they would bury their dead. They would weep for their friends for a day. A week. A month. And then they would put the deaths aside and go about as they were."

"This is true," Grey Wolf said.

"But hear me now, Grey Wolf. When you take a beloved as a captive and disappear into the night—when no one knows where that one is or are they alive? Those that care much for the missing one never stop weeping. They never stop looking. Hoping. The heart is broken every day. This is the kind of conquest that has no end. True, we cannot defeat the riders. But we can sadden their lives as they have saddened ours. They would break our hearts and spirits by placing us on a reservation. We will destroy their lives by taking those they love and hiding them away forever. We will take captives to sell in Mexico, trade for horses."

"But, who would we take? And how?" Buffalo Horn asked. Red Stick answered for Michael.

"We know the way. We take the yellow-haired woman and the boy. I have seen them through the medicine glasses. They are the ones we want. Any who try to stop us, we kill."

"No good!" Buffalo Horn cried. "Too many guns! Too many riders."

Now Red Stick spoke again.

"Hear me! Saturdays. Late in the day. All riders go to Travis. I have watched for many days. This is a big true. This is our time."

"What of the hairy one? And the Mexican? They are the real danger."

Red Stick smiled broadly. He was anticipating this very question.

"They are gone," he said. "I don't know where, but they left days ago. They left with kits for a long trip. Late on Saturday only a cook called Walter and an old drunk named Wind Walker. When they are dead there is no one to protect the woman and the boy."

The trio of lobos looked one each to the other. They turned in unison to their leader and nodded.

"I know Wind Walker. He was big medicine long ago. He killed many buffalos and blue coats too at Red River. Now he is broken. He drinks big whiskey. Never fight anymore. We go Saturday," Grey Wolf said with a wicked grin.

Chapter Fourteen
Broken Spur Ranch
October 1888

Walter Beasley had turned a section of the large Broken Spur kitchen into partial living quarters for himself. He very much preferred it to the rather smallish kitchen in the big house. It was true, he still slept in the big bunk house, but for washing himself and keeping his beard he found the nearness of hot water appealing.

Buckets of coal and bundles of kindling staves near the stove assured there would always be a huge kettle on the cookstove for the washing of the tin plates, cups, pots and pans that went along with meal preparation for the Spur riders.

He was rather proud of his salt and pepper beard, but he liked it neat and trimmed. He kept a pair of barber's shears and a large, old mirror in a corner of the kitchen just for that purpose. He reserved those sundown hours on Saturdays to trim his beard and hair, and generally bathe himself.

These were the hours the riders usually went to Travis for cards and a little beer drinking. Left alone, he was not subjected to the cat calls and profane whistles from the cowboys when they encountered him unclothed, standing in a steaming tub and cleansing his person.

This evening, as he removed his clothing and readied his bath, he noticed his mirror was heavily spotted with the greasy film that accumulated from time to time from the nearby cooking. He had submerged the glass into a large pan of soapy water and scrubbed its surface. He had just withdrawn it and was drying it, at the same time studying his naked reflection.

I'm still a purty good lookin' feller, he thought. *Might ought to get me a wife sometime.*

It was as he admired his likeness that he saw the reflection over his shoulder. Approaching him from the rear was a strange Indian with a large skinning knife held aloft.

A former soldier who had faced danger more times than he had wished and trained to fight, Walter spun around to face the intruder. Swinging the heavy mirror, he struck the stranger upside his head, nearly knocking him from his feet.

Walter lunged to the kitchen's butcher block and grasped a knife of his own. As he turned sideways to the trespasser, the Indian struck out with his blade in a sword-like thrust and sank his blade up to the hilt in Walter's armpit socket and into his chest cavity.

Almost at the same instant, Walter swung his own butcher's knife, striking deeply into the side of the interloper's neck, causing an immediate fountain of spurting blood. The trespasser cried out and attempted to staunch the flow of blood from his throat with his grasping hand as he fled the room.

Walter's wound began to take an effect upon him. First, he staggered a bit and then lost his footing. The wound was a deep one and blood flowed freely, staining Walter's nude body. As his strength ebbed, he called, "Wind Walker—Windy, you son of a bitch—Get in here!"

It was after the fourth call that Wind Walker appeared in the doorway of the kitchen. He was his usual disheveled self and a bit unsteady on his feet. Through bleary eyes he asked, "Whacha want, Walter? You been hurt? You cut ya self? You bleedin' pretty bad, ain'tcha."

"Fetch Colin!" Walter said. "Get Colin. Go now! Get him." His shouting made his wound hurt more. *Like fire*, he thought. *Hot—like fire.*

"Mister Colin," Wind Walker managed. "He ain't about. He's up and gone to Travis with all the boys. Big pool game. Ain't nobody here. Jus' me'n you. You need a rag 'er sumpin?"

"Get to Miss Pamela! Get up to the big house. Tell her, run! Leave the Spur. Tell her, run away! Get your ass out of here! Go tell her now!"

"You want I should bring her here?" Wind Walker was confused. *Walter never acted like this afore*, he thought.

"Hell no, you stupid drunk! This is a Comanche murder raid! Tell her to get the hell out of here. Tell her, run away! Take Little Buck and run! Go now! Right now!"

Wind Walker turned in the doorway and slumped away with a slight stagger. Walter wished that he had anyone for help right now except Wind Walker. He cursed himself for not having a gun. He tried to regain his footing.

He thought perhaps he could warn Pamela himself. The effort proved too much. He slumped to the floor again. A warm, black blanket spread over him, and he gave in to a comfortable, painless sleep.

Grey Wolf staggered his way to the tied horses. His throat bleeding badly, he sought help from his confederates. No one was attending the mounts though. Red Stick, Michael and Buffalo Horn had already crossed the front porch of the big house and were entering the foyer through the main door. The stairs to the second-floor bed chambers lay before them.

"Miss Pamela! Miss Pam! The" voice was at once loud and indistinct. "Walter says, you best run away! Walter says you run!"

It was an hour after sundown when Tom Arnette decided to make his evening rounds. As Constable of Travis, he felt it was his duty to check the locks on the storefronts after their closing time. He had never found an unlocked door, but nonetheless, he felt duty bound to look over the businesses on Pamela Street each night.

Because it was Saturday evening, it was not unusual to spot seven or eight horses tied to the hitching rail in front of the Staghorn Saloon since its reopening. This evening the horses were there as expected.

The one difference was the buckskin. He knew that horse belonged to Colin Trav. Everyone knew Colin rode a buckskin horse and he had for ten or more years. He and his yellow horse with the black mane and tail were close. Had the horse been a human, they might have been brothers.

It was no surprise to Arnette to see the horse. Colin came to town with the ranch hands from time to time, but considering the raid on the Prescott's, he felt Colin should have a warning. He stepped inside the batwing doors of the Staghorn and, catching Colin's eye while he stood at the end of the long bar, he motioned for him to step outside. Colin joined Tom Arnette on the boardwalk.

"How do, Tom?" Colin greeted his old friend. "What's new with you?"

"Colin, could you spare me a moment? Come along with me. I have something you need to see." Colin saw at once that the constable had something serious on his mind.

"Sure, Tom. Lead the way."

Arnette escorted Colin a few doors down the street to the Constable's office. Once inside, he ushered his old boss through a door in the rear of the building and into the jail cell section. Colin saw that on the floor of the nearest cell a sheet of canvas was covering something. Arnette withdrew the covering and revealed the burned and twisted bodies that had been brought to him earlier.

"Gawd damn, Tom," Colin exclaimed. "What the hell happened here? These poor folks. Who are they?"

"It's what's left of the Prescott family, I think. I think that's Edmond, his wife and little boy, Junie."

"What in the name of God happened to them?" Colin was having trouble keeping his stomach from turning over.

"I ain't sure what happened. Uncle Ike Pauley says it's the devilment of a Comanche war party. He says they even killed the cow—a dog too, I guess. I'm going out to their place tomorrow and see if I can tell anymore about it. But I think you'd do well to cinch up and ride home."

"You're thinkin' whoever did this is still around?"

"I know nothing for sure, except they—whoever they is—wanted horses and guns bad enough to kill these folks and burn the homestead."

"Burned 'em out too? That's why they look like this?"

"Uncle Ike dug 'em out of the ashes and brought 'em here. I got to figure out how and where I'm going to bury them. I didn't know them hardly at all. Thing is, you got a passel of horse flesh out to the Spur. I imagine you got a gun or two. If I was you, I'd get home. Maybe no trouble at all. But, still...."

Back at the Staghorn, Colin thought about taking Justin and Bobby Baxter with him. Upon reflection he decided there probably was no immediate danger. After all, the Prescott farm was more than twenty miles away. Besides, the pool tournament was in full swing, and the boys were whooping it up pretty good. The cowhands had planned this night of revelry for a very long time.

Still, he thought his place was at the ranch with Pamela and his son. With his desire to be home clouding his judgement, he cinched his saddle and rode off through the dark, alone. His horse, Buck, instinctively knew the way. Colin trusted this big stallion as he had for years. He relaxed to the smooth short lope of his mount and, except for thoughts of the Prescott's, the ride through the night air was a pleasant one.

Headed west by southwest to the Spur, faint starlight and a quarter moon provided a dim glow along his path. As he turned into the lane that led the last half mile to the house, a lone figure, partially hidden by the brush edging the lane, pointed a Winchester 73 at the silhouette of the mounted man heading his direction.

Red Stick had no way of knowing in the semi-darkness who he was shooting at. He knew only that he and his band of lobos had hard work ahead of them this night and they needed no interference. The 44-caliber bullet did its assigned work.

Knocking Colin from the saddle completely, the bullet entered the right side of his chest. Seeing the rider fall and that he no longer posed a threat, Red Stick hurried back to the side of his band. Colin neither heard the shot nor felt the blow. He only knew he was falling from the saddle.

Damn it, he thought. *I haven't fell off a horse since I was six years old. What's the matter with me, Buck?* These thoughts were replaced by a sleepiness Colin had never felt before. He realized he was holding the leather reins still in his grasp.

Just stand easy, Buck. I'll get up in a minute... just a little dizzy... need get on home. And then he was asleep. Colin lay still in the dust of the lane. His horse Buck nuzzled his face and was confused as to why his pal was so still.

A few people in the surrounding area heard the rifle report in the darkness. It concerned no one. Nighttime gunshots were often heard in areas where settlers kept chickens and an abundant population of coyotes coveted them.

Pamela Trav was undressing and readying herself for bed. It was earlier than usual for her to retire, but it had been a trying day. She disliked it when the entire crew of the Spur went off to town together. Especially, when Colin went along with them. The vastness of the ranch was just too silent. Too ominous. She also chose to arm herself when left alone with only her son, ten-year-old Buck, as a companion.

"Get yourself ready for bed now, Buck," Pamela told her son.

"Momma, I need to use the outhouse first."

"It's pretty dark out there. You sure you wouldn't want to just use the chamber pot?"

"Shoot, Momma, I ain't afraid of the dark."

"Alright. I guess you are Momma's big man at that. You go out through the kitchen and grab a couple of matches. There's a new candle in the privy. I put it there this morning. Use the candle—be sure you blow it out when you come to the house."

"Okay, Momma." Without another word he was out the door and down the stairs.

He's sure getting to be a big boy, Pamela thought. *Doesn't want to potty in front of his Mom.*

Since their wedding ten years ago, Colin had kept a huge Walker Colt pistol in one of the dresser drawers. It was a remnant of bygone days of a Texas under the protection of the Rangers. Captain Samuel Harrison Walker had made the pistol famous as the favorite assault weapon of the mounted Ranger.

The old gun still worked as if it were new, although it was now considered a relic. Still this six-pound gigantic pistol had the power of a stick of dynamite.

Colin had purchased the old gun at an auction for a dollar. He was impressed by its heft and enjoyed looking from time to time at the old antique. He kept the big cap and ball gun loaded, but he and Pamela never really thought they might ever need it.

"'Sides that," Colin had allowed. "Any bandit sees the size of that gun, it'll probably scare him off anyways."

Fully charged with powder and ball, it was the most powerful revolver of its time. Pamela withdrew the weighty pistol from the drawer and laid it on her bed. As she continued preparing for bed, she was interrupted by a voice coming from the rear grass patch of the house. It sounded as though it was directly under her partially opened window.

"Miss Pam," The unsteady voice continued, "Miss Pamela."

That's old Wind Walker, she thought. *What in the Lord's name could he be hollerin' about?*

Coincidently, Wind Walker's ruckus also alerted the three invaders slipping into the doorway. Red Stick peered out into the darkness in the direction of the voice and saw a flicker of candle glow emerging from the outdoor privy shack. The convenience shed stood forty yards from the front and slightly to the side of the household.

"Be silent now," Michael, the white warrior, whispered. "Someone's there. Coming this way." When the approaching figure had taken a few more steps, he fell into a slight glow from a kerosene lantern in Pamela's upstairs' window.

"It's the boy!" whispered Michael. "It's the one we came for."

"Grab him!" Red Stick ordered. "Get him, Michael. Grab him—Don't stop. Get him on your horse with you and ride. Go the way we said. Buffalo and me, we'll get the woman. We'll meet you at the big pond where we were last night. Don't kill him—Don't let him get away. Tie him when you can. Don't stop though, till you're away from here."

Obeying Red Stick's orders, Michael broke away from the group and ran toward the slight form. Racing through the darkness, Michael swiftly scooped the startled youngster into his arms. Ten-year-old Buck Trav yelled loudly in surprise and struggled.

Only a few yards away now, Wind Walker, startled senseless by the happenings in the dark, also cried out.

The boy, Buck, still struggling, called out loudly. He thrashed wildly against the sinewy arms of the marauder, clawing at Michael's face. At last, feeling he was about to lose his grip on the youngster, Michael swung his fist in a mighty arc against the side of the boy's head causing his right eye to swell nearly shut almost instantly.

"Silence—quiet or I kill you," he whispered to the boy. The blow stunned Buck so badly he nearly blacked out. Head swimming, he was resigned now that he could not escape. He allowed himself to be carried to the waiting horses. Sobbing softly in the hard grip of the raider, in an instant he and his captor sat astride Edmond Prescott's stolen broodmare. Caution to the wind, they raced wildly into the darkness.

Pamela, now certain there was something dreadfully wrong and her son was in danger, grabbed the big Colt and walked out of the bedroom to the head of the stairway. Alerted as she was and filled with terror and desperation for her son, she overlooked her nudity. She sensed—knew—there was a real danger here. First, she had heard Wind Walker and now her son was crying out. In Comanche country this amounted to a frantic alert.

With Red Stick leading the way, he and Buffalo Horn were only three steps from the top of the stairs. Red Stick had been watching his feet as he ascended the stairs. Now, he raised his head and saw he was only four feet away from an unclothed white woman.

More than a woman at this moment, she was a mountain lion. His surprised reaction was all it took for Pamela to thumb back the hammer on the big pistol and, supporting its formidable weight with both hands, attempted to shoot Red Stick squarely in the face.

The deafening explosion of the heavy revolver filled the air in the stairwell with a huge billow of white smoke and a myriad of flecks of flaming gunpowder. The Walker's massive recoil nearly wrenched the gun from Pamela's grip. The heavy bullet flew by the leader's left ear by a mere inch. It struck Buffalo Horn instead—in exactly the spot Pamela had intended for Red Stick.

Buffalo Horn's head exploded like a ripe melon, and his body was driven completely over the stairway's banister by the heavy lead ball. The kidnapper crashed to the floor in the downstairs hall, overturning a lamp table and the hall tree.

Red Stick, though, did not completely escape the devastation of the massive explosion. The airborne charge of gunpowder hit him full in the face creating a massive burn and at the same time, burying dozens of flaming black powder grains under the skin of his face. Holding his scorched face, he reeled and fell backwards rolling end over end completely to the foot of the stair.

In a final moment of defiance and through the ravages of pain, he managed to free his tomahawk from his belt and hurled it towards Pamela with all the strength he had left. The axe, thrown in desperation, could have struck anywhere, but Red Stick's instincts were truer than he imagined.

The blade of the light axe struck Pamela at the lower corner of her right eye. From there it slashed its way downward to the center of her upper lip and buried more than an inch of its edge into her cheek bone. In pain and shock, she collapsed on the floor of the upper hall. Red

Stick, through his searing agony, made his way to his waiting horse. Spurring the animal as hard as he might, he sped away at full tilt into the night.

Red Stick was a half mile in the dark behind the warrior, Michael, who held the boy tightly in his arms and drove his mount relentlessly until the mare fairly flew through the darkness. Behind him and nearly covered in blood—barely able to stay in the saddle—was the would-be assassin, Grey Wolf. Near death, weakened and light-headed from blood loss, the raider had been seriously wounded by the butcher knife of Walter Beasley.

Red Stick's face burned as he raced headlong into the darkness. The sortie had been a failure, not at all the way he had pictured it.

But we have the boy, he thought. *At least, we have the boy. Perhaps I've killed the woman. I think I struck her well with the tomahawk.*

CHAPTER FIFTEEN
The Day After the Raid
October 1888

"Just where do you think that Walter is?" Robert asked angrily. He and Juan Garcia had been sitting in the passenger car in the same place they were hitched to the locomotive engine only a few days before, for more than two hours.

"Perhaps he did not receive the wire," Garcia answered. "Might be that Sheriff Tom didn't get it or he forgot to tell Walter about it."

"I really ain't in the mood for a long hike to the Spur, but I'd guess we might just as well get at it." It was at that moment that the same young man who had directed them to board the car when they departed came from the western direction of the rails and was heading their way, driving a shafted flat wagon drawn along by a large roan mare.

"Is that there a buckboard I spy?" Robert asked.

"Si, Si," this from Garcia. "We may have found a ride after all."

"Not may have—Damn sure have!" Robert responded. "Pull up there, young feller. We's needin' a lift over to Travis and out to the Broken Spur Ranch. Can you haul us?"

"'Fraid not," the boy answered. "I got to be gettin' this here wagon up to the section gang. They's about two or three miles up the line. I'm right sorry, I am."

"What's your name, son?" Garcia asked.

"Irish," the young man responded. "Folks all just call me Irish."

"Well, here's the way it sets, Señor Irish. Either you're going to haul us over to our ranch or I'm gonna kick your ass off that wagon and I'll do the driving myself. How would it best suit you?"

The darkness in Garcia's eyes and his steady voice told the youngster he was meeting a serious man. Further, he spied the revolver in the Mexican's sash.

"Which way is this here ranch, anyhow?"

"Just beyond Travis a few miles."

"Give me a minute to turn Gussy around. I guess the railroad folks would probably want me to help out. You bein' a customer and all."

The trip to the Spur was made mostly in silence and took just a shade less than three hours. When the trio was within the last half mile of the big house, Garcia asked, "Do you see that little dust cloud up ahead?"

"I sure do. I know who it is, too. It's Bobby and Rocket. Man alive, that boy loves that old roan. Fastest horse around too."

"I remember when you gave him that horse. Just a two-year-old then," Garcia reminisced.

"Wasn't much of a gift. As I recall nobody else could ride the damn fool thing. Just wilder than a buck deer."

"Bobby was too. Wild I mean. How long ago?" Garcia was thoughtful.

"Been seven or eight years, I'm sure. Maybe longer. Bobby and Rocket—still together. Makes you think, don't it?"

Bobby Baxter reined in Rocket to a stop beside the flat wagon. His excitement as he related the happenings of the night before at the ranch house made him almost incoherent.

"Gawd damn—slow yourself!" Robert demanded. "Is anybody dead? Who did all this devilment anyhow?"

"Wind Walker said it was a Comanche lobo, name of Red Stick."

"Wind Walker?" Garcia asked. "Was he sober enough to know what he saw?"

"Told me Walter sent him to warn Miss Pam. That's when he sees this here Red Stick. He says he knowed Red Stick from when he used to be one of the Quahadi. Wind Walker is a Kiowa, but they rode together all the time, I think. Red Stick and his gang must have broken out of the reservation. Makin' war on his own. Windy says when they're out on their own, they's called lobos. Wolves, Wind Walker says. He might have been pretty drunk alright. I think seeing what was goin' on probably sobered him some. We need to be gettin' up to the house, though. Miss Pam—she sorely wounded. Walter and Mister Colin both near death. And they runned off with Little Buck! Just awful. I'm sure glad y'all are home. We just only got that wire you sent this morning from Sheriff Arnette."

Robert and Garcia exchanged glances.

"Justin's right behind me," Baxter said. "He was hitching a team to come for you. Bringin' the flat wagon, so's to fetch your bags along."

"Alright, Irish. You can unload us and turn your wagon around now," Robert said. "Ye can get back to that section gang. Here's for your trouble." Robert slipped a gold coin from his pocket and into the hand of Irish O'Flynn.

"You don't have to fetch me this much," the youngster said. "Ten dollars is a way too much."

"On your way, Mick," Garcia spoke up. "Better beat it with his money afore he changes his mind." The two alighted from Irish's wagon and prepared to wait for Justin and the second wagon.

Doctor Reuben Pritchard was bending over Colin when Robert and Juan entered the second-story bedroom that was now a hospital for both Colin and Pamela. The doctor was attempting to slow the flow of blood from a wound on the right side of Colin's chest.

"Hello Robert, Garcia." The doctor whispered. "Sure glad to see you boys are home. Colin's sprung a little leak here. I'm stopping it up now for the third time."

"Is he going to make it, Doc?" Robert asked.

Garcia stood by Robert's side as stoic as an oak. The men held their voices low.

"Well, he's in sorry shape now. If I can get him to stop losing blood, he's got a real good chance. Big bullet. Tore a hell of a hole. Went clear through and through. That's good, except I got a hole in the front and back too. Seems I plug one and the other wants to leak. Been fighting this for couple of hours now. But, as to your question—Yes, I think he'll pull through. I can't say the same for Walter, though. He's been stabbed so near the heart, an inch deeper and he'd already be dead. He's touch and go. Pamela there…" he gestured toward the second bed that had been set up in the master bedroom. "Pamela has a terrible wound. Took a passel of stitching up, I'll tell you. She ain't in danger of dying, but it's going to be a long spell before I want her out of bed."

"Oh, my beautiful Pammy." Robert was wiping tears with a red bandanna. He studied the face he thought so lovely, now swaddled in a massive mound of white bandages.

"I know she looks like hell," Reuben Pritchard went on. "She can't hear you. Her pain must just be something awful. I've got her so full of laudanum she's going to sleep a long while. Walter's in the front bedroom downstairs."

"That's my room," Robert said. "I'm glad he's in there. It's a comfortable spot. Big windows. Cool air most of the time."

"You can look in on him. He isn't going to know you're there. He's sleeping pretty deep. Some, because of the sleeping elixir I mixed up, but mostly because of all the blood he's missing. Lots of it inside his chest. If you don't mind, I'd just as soon you let him be for a day or two. You probably want to talk to Wind Walker. He saw most of this trouble happening."

"Reckon he's sober enough to know anything?" Garcia asked.

"Oh, you can bet he's sober. Bobby Baxter has him locked in the bunkhouse. I'm sure he'd like a little drink, but that's not going to happen. Least ways, not any time soon. Bobby's determined to keep him dry until we get the whole story. At least as well as Old Windy can tell anything."

"I don't want to speak with him," Garcia said. "I might kill him. He could have fought these bandidos. He could have at least tried. He should be dead because he fought but he is alive because he did not. I'm sure he was drunk. Too drunk to fight. I should not like to see him. Not now. I only want to hear about this Red Stick."

Doctor Pritchard sat on the edge of the bed. He had worked many hours over the three injured and was approaching exhaustion.

"Renegade Comanche, Wind Walker says. Lobos, they call them. Out to steal horses, guns, whatever."

"How many in the party?" Robert asked.

"Well, Pamela killed one of them. Walter had a bloody butcher knife when we found him. We figure he put up a fight. Hurt somebody, we think. We think it was a small party. Maybe four or five. That's all we know."

"Doc, I can't tell you how glad I am that you're here. You tell that brother of yours to go ahead and build his bank. Tell him I'll sign the papers when we get back." Robert said.

"Get back? You just got here! Where are you going off to now?"

"I'm going to go get my grandson. Where the hell would you think?"

"With what I told you about your heart?"

"Just keep that to yourself. I got business elsewhere."

As the two strode from the house, Garcia was stopped by Long John Barlow. As Robert walked on and out of earshot, Long John told Garcia something that was obviously important, but not for the ears of Robert Trav. Garcia seemed to thank Barlow for the private information, then hurried to Robert's side.

*   *   *

Bobby Baxter was more than ready for the chase. Justin was at his side, checking the opened loading gate on the cylinder of his Colt.

"We'll get some horses ready, Mister Robert. The boys are rarin' to go too. We had a hard time keepin' them here. Just wanted to hear from you first. See what you thought we should do. They got six, maybe seven, hours on us, but we can run 'em down."

"Just two mounts. No riders. None!" Garcia spoke through clenched teeth. "Saddle Punkin for Mister Robert. My pinto gelding for me. Saddlebags—couple of blankets. Ponchos. Rifle scabs."

"You two ain't goin' alone?" Justin asked.

"That's how it is." Robert Trav's voice was hard as iron. "You two need to be right here. This all could be a trick, don't you know? Small party, just three or four slips in here and raises some hell. Gets every fightin' man within twenty miles chasin' after 'em. This here Red Stick and his boys might just be a couple of scouts for a big war party. Big murder and burn raid might be yet to come."

"How do you know we were hit by a small party?" Baxter asked.

"'Cause Pamela and Walter are still alive. 'Cause this here house is still standin'. Was this a scalp hunt, wouldn't be nobody livin'. This house'd be charcoal. Just the two of us will be taking up this chase. No more."

"But, Papaw," Justin wheedled. "That's my brother out there. Just you and Garcia? Are you sure about this?"

"I know what you're thinking. Can two old men handle this bunch? Let me tell you something you'll learn yourself as time goes by. When you're young—like you and Bobby here…When you're young, you're strong and tough. When you get old—like me 'n Garcia—you may not be strong and tough anymore. But now you're mean and dirty. When we catch this here Red Stick outlaw—and you can be sure we will—when we catch up to him, if he's 'spectin' a fair fight, he's in for one hell of a big revelation. I'm just hopin' we don't have to shoot him."

"Why would you hope that?" Baxter asked.

"'Cause I want to hang the son of a bitch, that's why. I want to see how he likes white man justice. When we get him, he can give his soul to his Great Spirit, but you can bet his ass belongs to me. Me and Garcia. 'Sides that, these brigands get the notion that a big party's following them, they'll kill Little Buck for sure. Might happen just with Johnny and me too."

"Guess I never thought of that," Baxter said.

Now Garcia added, "They'll leave his body for us to find. Take our attention away from them and suck us into an ambush. Better they don't know we're after 'em, till we can catch 'em off guard. Hit 'em all at once before they can think what to do. Ambush on our side if we can set one up."

Robert was growing impatient. "It's sure the truth I want to catch these bastards and I'm willing to kill all of 'em. Most of all though, I want my grandson back. You boys ain't comin' along and that's that. The more of us there is, the better chance them renegades got of spottin' us. No more talk now. Bobby, get them horses like Garcia told you. Justin, you go out to the ranch kitchen. Fix us up a couple of pokes of grub. Cold stuff we can eat 'thout no cookin'. Some eggs, some smoked ham, too. Any tins of sardines or salmon would be good. If you spot any cornbread, cold flap jacks fetch it along. There's canned peaches out there, too. 'Nuff for three, four days. Then get up to the house. Bring your daddy's Henry rifle and see can you find me a pistol of some kind."

"Yes, sir. We all want Little Buck back more'n anything too," Justin answered. "Want your old Hawken, Papaw?" He was referring to the beloved, old flintlock rifle Robert had carried when he was a trapper in the Rockies.

"Leave the Hawken. Too heavy. Cain't hold it up no more."

"Mister Robert," Bobby had his hat in his hand. "If there ain't no changing your mind 'bout us going along with you, would it be alright if I brought Lisa out here for a while? She could help tendin' to Mister Colin and Miss Pamela. Walter, too. 'Sides, with renegades afoot, I don't like her being alone and all. Even in town."

"You want to bring your little tavern gal out here, do ya?"

"She ain't a tavern girl because she wants to be. She's just kind of stuck in a hard spot. Least ways, for now."

"Bobby, you're the top hand of this outfit. You're the straw boss. You're supposed to be the brains of this here outfit. If you think the smart thing to do is to bring her out here, it's your call. You rescuin' her from a life of sin? That's right worthy, Bobby. When she steals your watch and breaks your heart, I ain't gonna say I told you so. Well—maybe I will. Bring her out. Watch our silverware, though. Now, you fetch them horses up. Move your asses a little."

"*Bien vomos! Date prisa!*" Garcia added

In less than a half an hour both horses, fully saddled and outfitted, were brought forward. Garcia's spotted gelding snorted in glad recognition when he spotted the *vaquero*. Punkin, saddled for Robert, was a light-colored bay Morgan horse mare with a roached mane and a flaxen, half tail.

Pamela had bought the six-year-old Morgan brood mare from the Vermont area where this all-purpose breed originated in the late 1700s by breeder, music teacher and town clerk, Justin Morgan. She was a promising mare as a buggy-driving horse and a breeder, but she truly shined as a saddle mount. As sturdy as a draft breed, yet whirlwind swift, Garcia thought the easy-going personality made the Morgan a good choice for Old Robert. In an instant Garcia swung into his saddle. For Robert the effort was greater and slower. Still, he mounted his leathery chair without help. Garcia offered a curt, "Adios" to the watching Justin and Bobby.

"Let's ride, Johnny," came from Robert.

The two cowboys stood side by side in the front yard of the big house and watched as the pair of old men short loped their mounts away to the south and west in the direction of the river.

"I love that old man, Bobby. I love them both. I just wonder if I'll ever see them alive again."

Uncontrollably, Justin's tears stained his cheeks.

"I'll bet we do," Bobby Baxter answered. "That's one hell of a pair. Bet Red Stick sees 'em too."

CHAPTER SIXTEEN
On the Trail
October 1888

Red Stick, his face on fire from the black powder burns, spurred the stolen horse hard. As his mount ran blindly through the darkness, he hoped he was somewhat following Michael and the kidnapped boy. They had agreed to rendezvous at a large pothole out deep in the high grass of the Llano Escatado. It was a place they both knew. They had spent the previous night there as they had laid out the plans for the raid on the Broken Spur. The raid had not proceeded as the four kidnappers had laid out.

Buffalo Horn dead, Red Stick said to himself. *I am burned with the gun powder of an old Ranger pistol. Was Grey Wolf wounded?* He had caught a glimpse of Grey Wolf as he rode out ahead and he seemed slumped over the neck of his horse.

I wouldn't be surprised if he was dead, too. This whole thing should not have gone so badly. They had no idea that we were coming. We have good horses—good guns. We have the boy at least. The woman may die. My axe was true. All would have been better if we could have taken her alive."

Once he entered the tall grass of the Escatado, his horse had to slow. No horse could run at top speed in the heavy cover. Nonetheless, Red Stick used the cavalry spurs to keep the mount moving as fast as possible. Both Red Stick and Michael had given up the soft deerskin footwear of the Comanche for the boots and spurs of the pony soldier. How Michael had acquired cavalry boots was unknown to Red Stick.

His own came about by an act of Comanche heroism. Red Stick, under the cover of night, had slipped into a cavalry bivouac area and stolen the boots he now wore from a sleeping trooper. He had slipped out of the area without awakening a single soul. It was a deed akin to the counting of coup, a remarkable feat of stealth and bravery.

Later, when he had stood before a council fire and told the story of the boots and how he obtained them, the old men of the Quahadi lauded his courage and had rewarded his courage with the dried foot of a red-tailed hawk. Its talons clenched and suspended on a necklace of glass beads which he wore even now as one of his most prized possessions.

A faint glow of starlight reflected on the surface of the pond in the grass, and he knew he was nearing the meeting place. He dismounted his hard-breathing horse. Leading his mount by the bridle, he made his way to the edge of the pond. The two lobos greeted each other with whispers. With only faint starlight to counter the total blackness, Red Stick could just make out the shapes in the gloom of his squad. In a while, his eyes became more acclimated to the gloom and now he could better identify the figures.

Michael was directly in front of him squatting near the pond's edge. The boy sat beside Michael with his arms around drawn-up knees. He was sobbing noticeably.

"*Silencio!*" Red Stick rasped in a loud whisper. He had learned the white men he encountered understood the language of the Mexican far better than the guttural sounds of the Quahadi. Like all Comanche, Kiowa and Apache, he had dealt with Mexicans many times along the Rio Grande. He had met with them in trade sometimes. Other times in war. He had learned enough words he could deal with them.

Red Stick leaned forward and delivered a sharp slap to the boy's face. Young Buck Trav uttered a small gasp at the pain of the slap and then grew silent, stifling his sobs he forbade himself to cry. He knew Colin would not cry. Bobby Baxter would never cry. There was just enough light that Michael saw what had happened. In a flash, he grabbed at Red Stick's shirt and spun him about.

"Strike that boy again and I'll kill you." Michael's voice was cold and dangerous. Red Stick backed away at the same time withdrawing another tomahawk from his belted waist.

"Say what you mean," Red Stick demanded. "I am the leader here. You play a dangerous game, Michael."

"You're a fool, Red Stick. You have a captive worth a hundred horses. Like all Comanche, all you can think of is torture—murder. Apache, too. When you have a precious thing, all you know is to kill it."

"That is our way. What is this precious thing? This boy? He is the precious thing? What do we do? Sell him to the Comancheros?" Red Stick was becoming precariously impatient. Anger was welling within him.

"Not Comancheros. They would want the boy and that's a fact for sure. They would take him in a minute—then kill us both and ride away with him."

"Mexico, then?" Red Stick ventured.

"If you tried to make a trade with Mexicans, it would go the same way. You and I dead, our captive would be theirs. No. The right place to sell this captive is back to the people we took him from. They have many horses. Many dollars. They will pay one thousand dollars for him. No—two thousand! They will not pay if he is dead. He must not be injured—not tortured—your people's way or not. He is *our* way to finding more warriors—foxes and wolves—to join us. If we can pay, we will have a fine war party. More raids. Horses, gold—Mexican señoritas. We can drive the whites north from here."

In the dark Red Stick could not see the excitement on Michael's face, but he could hear it—feel it in his voice.

"But, I think the ones we stole him away from are on our trail now. If the riders catch up with us—well, they are many. The fight would be a poor one."

"I don't think they are many," Michael said. "I think they are three, maybe four. I think they keep the most riders to guard the home. It's what I would do. You would, too."

"Yes. That is wise." Red Stick was thoughtful now. "They don't know if we are many. If all the men left to chase us, it would be easy for some of us to slip back and torch everything. You are wise, Michael. We must kill the ones who are trailing us then."

"No. Kill all, but one. One must be left alive to go back and tell the others of how to get the boy back."

"I see. But, then how do we make the trade for money. Won't they come with many riders, kill us and take the boy? How does your plan work now?"

"I don't know yet. We must first let those who follow us know they are in danger. I must think."

As they had spoken the sun had just begun to rise a bit and Red Stick noticed a long form lying at Michaels feet.

"Is that Grey Wolf? Is he alive?"

"No, he is dead. He will be the bait for our trap to kill those who hunt us."

It was near noon of the second day as Robert slid from his saddle and began to walk alongside his horse. Garcia, being to the rear noticed a large wet spot on the seat of the old man's riding pants.

"Patron," he cried out. "Why are you walking?"

Old Robert turned and faced his friend. His expression was one of pain and dismay.

"It's my butt," he said. "Seems my ass is afire. I ain't rode a horse in 'bout thirty years and now I recall why."

Garcia took the reins from the hands of his compadre in in an instant had secured both mounts to a sturdy bush.

"Drop your pants, Robert," he commanded.

"Do what?" Robert was incredulous at this demand.

"Lower your britches and turn around. I would see why you have a wet seat." Seeing that Robert was hesitant to his order, Garcia repeated himself more emphatically. "Down! Pants down!"

At last, Robert reluctantly lowered his riding trousers to mid-thigh. Garcia was at his rear.

"Trap door too." Garcia voiced. He could already see the that spot on Robert's cotton underwear was blood.

"Ain't no way I can reach back there and unlatch them buttons. You gonna make me fall right on my kisser."

In a moment Garcia had released the three small buttons that secured the convenient opening in the rear of the union suit. Then he saw the abrasion.

"Ah caramba," he exclaimed. "Mi amigo! You have a saddle sore the size of my fist and it's raw and leaking." Garcia was visibly upset.

"Well, guess I'll have to hoof it from here on in." Robert's voice was shaky and unsure.

Garcia understood immediately that traversing this land afoot was death sentence. In this wild country a man must ride or die.

"I have something in my saddle bag that will help you, I think. I have a strong horse liniment. It will seal off the blood. Help with the hurting a little, I think. Seems to on a horse anyway."

"You say horse liniment? You going to put horse liniment on my ass? I ain't so sure about that, Juan. Probably going to burn, too, don't you think?"

"Si. Burn like fires of hell but we must try. After burn, though, it'll feel better. I'll tear up a blanket and try to pad your leather. You cannot stay afoot here. You must ride Robert. If it is pain, you must stand it. You can't walk. Not from here."

True to Garcia's prediction, the liniment burned like a live coal. Also as foretold, the blood leaking from the abrasion halted. Now Garcia retrieved a wicked-looking, large pocketknife and carefully cut the entire seat from Roberts rugged, canvas trousers. Now, he sliced off the trap door portion of the cotton undergarment leaving Robert's buttocks exposed and with nothing in friction with the garish wound.

"Am I to go about with mine arse ashine?" Robert wanted to know.

"Just give me another minute," was Garcia's retort. "I'm doing the best that I can. Once we're back to the ranch we can do better."

"That's when and if we get back."

Garcia spent the next few minutes cutting up a blanket and padding Robert's saddle. Then he cut a small skirt from the same blanket and fixed it about Robert's waist.

"So now it's a little dress you want me to wear, is it?"

"Stop the complaining, damn it! You're a Scot. Think of it as a kilt."

Robert stirrupped his left foot and, using all his remaining strength, he pulled himself into the saddle. He was expecting a bolt of pain when his buttocks met the saddle seat but surprisingly the pad than Garcia had fashioned from the blanket was indeed soft and comfortable. Also, the liniment now had lost its intense burn and the pain relief was just setting in. Robert was nearly pain free.

"Ah," was his first word. "This is the best I've felt for two days. Sure, and I can think of my little skirt as a kilt. But it's still much like a little ladies dress."

Garcia gave a grunt. "Let us see if you can ride a bit now. Our quarry has gained some time on us.

The next day they found the dead man.

At the end of the third day in the saddle, Robert was amazed that he felt as well as he did. He had used two of his nitroglycerin tablets and, though he had a slight tightness in his breast, his chest felt better than his rump. His seat was still a bit saddle sore but, all in all, he had made it a full three days astride his mount right alongside Garcia.

Without extra horses they knew they had to make their mounts last for what could be a very long, arduous journey. Buffalo grass and grama were both plentiful and the pothole ponds provided plenty of water. The most important challenge was the exhaustion of their horses.

Each knew that a man on foot would never accomplish their goal of rescuing Little Buck. Also, without a horse, a man might easily perish in this wild country. They settled on a plan to ride for about an hour, then dismount and lead the steeds for twenty or thirty minutes. They would break their pace two or three times daily for a longer rest and to eat sparingly of their trail food.

"I make it to be four horses," Robert said. "The horseman in the front is leading the second horse. See how orderly their tracks are right together. I'm thinking whoever is leading this party is leading a horse that my grandson is on. The other two riders are loose, wandering. Horses are all wearing shoes. Those are mister Prescott's horses, I'm thinking."

The trail left by Red Stick's party was scant. They had skirted the heavy grass now as the trail made by saddle horses was too easy to follow through the crushed grama. Surrounding the heavy grass was a very unusual and rare thicket of cottonwood and mulberry. This was indeed providing more cover and making a more difficult trail for the pursuers.

Most would have lost the trail and abandoned the search after the first few miles. Robert Trav and Juan Garcia, though, were equally experienced in the out-of-doors and each of them had tracked wayward calves or stray horses for a major part of their lives. Occasionally, the Red Stick party's trail would vanish. The sharp eyes of the two hunters, though, would inevitably pick it up again and the pursuit would continue.

Late in the afternoon of the fourth day, as they reached the top of a small hillock, Robert gave Garcia a signal to be silent. Each man slid quietly from his saddle to the ground, reined his mount and crept soundlessly to the top of the rise.

Garcia's horse was extremely well-trained and as long as one of the reins lay on the ground, the pinto would not move even if there was gunfire. Robert lacked that confidence in Punkin and elected to tether her to a small, but sturdy, bush. From the top of the rise, they could look down into a clearing two hundred yards in front of them.

"Look, Patron," Garcia said. "They have left us something to look at. Tell me what do you see?"

"Well, it appears to be a dead Indian stretched out on the ground beside a pretty good horse. I think it's a catfish restin' on the pan of a steel trap," Robert mused. "Awfully decent of him to stretch out and die in plain view where we'd have no trouble eyeballing him. Prime cut of bait, don't you think?"

"Si, Patron. Nice of him to die out in the open, so we can just walk up to him and look him over and take his horse."

"I'm thinkin' with that one dead, there's just two lobos out there. Two and my grandson. I am further thinkin' that those two both have rifles trained on that dead body. Whosoever goes near that corpse is likely to join him."

"Do you think they are together?" Garcia asked. "Side by side?"

"No. I'd expect they're smarter than to let us catch 'em in a bunch. They've got good rifles, I think. Prescott's Winchester, anyway. Two-hundred-yard shot would be about all they could manage. Sun'll be settin' in another hour."

"That cuts the range to fifty. They'll be slipping in closer pretty soon, I think."

After several minutes of thought, Robert asked, "Do you think you could get that horse of yours to run down there to that dead Indian?"

Garcia was thoughtful. "Not the Indian. Diablo will go to the loose horse though, I think."

"Do you see what I'm thinkin? They see an empty horse they're maybe gonna think we're hurt. Or afoot. Or just too old to keep up the chase. See Garcia, that's an advantage to bein' old. Everybody thinks you can't do a damn thing and you're always in trouble. These lobos are thinking we're sure to come and look that dead Indian over. When we don't, and they see your horse with no rider, they just might think we're in trouble and they should come lookin' for the easy killin' of two old men. What do you think? Can we turn this ambush around?"

"I think we can hide in the brush by your horse, and they will come. More horses and more guns if they kill us, I think they will come. But what about the boy? What if they kill him, before they come for us?"

"Well, maybe I'm giving them too much credit. I sure hope not. I don't think they'll kill Little Buck. He's too valuable. Big ransom. Comancheros would pay up for him. Dead, he ain't worth nothin'. 'Course, they may decide to ransom right back to us. That's really the smart thing to do. I don't think they're stupid enough just to throw him away."

"It is risky, Patron. Comanches are big on torture and murder."

"I'm hoping they'll decide to torture and murder us instead, and sell the boy to the highest bidder," Robert answered wryly.

"Of the years we have saddled together, I have thought many times you would get me killed. All is the same. After all these years, all is the same. You're still trying to get me killed. Anyways, I'm going to slip down the slope a little and see if I can spot anything. I think there's enough trees and brush to cover me. You got your watch?"

"Yeah." Robert took the watch from his vest pocket. "Four thirty, it says."

"At five-thirty, turn my horse loose. I think he'll go to that horse by the dead man. Crawl back in the brush with your rifle and just wait. It is a good idea they should come to look for us when they see Diablo's loose. If the boy isn't with them, take any shot you get. No missing!"

CHAPTER SEVENTEEN
October 1888

"My squad found two dead men west of here about twenty miles. You being the nearest town, I thought you might know who they are. Might have family who'd want the bodies."

The young cavalry captain stood rigid as he addressed Sheriff Arnette. Arnette could not keep from noticing the young man's uniform was spotless and neatly pressed. Boots were glossy black. His horse was well groomed and the three privates with him were as neatly turned out as he was.

"I have the bodies over in the supply wagon." He motioned towards the smallish covered wagon and the two-horse team drawing it.

The citizens of Travis had begun to trickle out of their storefronts and shops to view the rarity of a visiting cavalry squad. They stood on the board sidewalks, their inquisitive faces alight with curiosity. Whatever was serious enough to bring army troops to Travis told them a tragedy must have occurred.

"Seems like folks keep bringin' their dead to me," Arnette said. "Place used to be a sheriff's office. It's more like a funeral parlor these days."

"West of here there's a large spring-fed pond. These two was camped there, it appears."

"Yeah. Folks around here call that place the big spring."

Arnette followed the captain to the supply wagon. When he looked inside, he saw the bodies of two men covered with army white tent canvas. As the captain drew the canvas aside, he saw a blonde, flat top guitar lying between them.

Instantly, he recognized it as the guitar the girl in the Staghorn had played. He knew it was Jesse Taylor's guitar. The two men were hardly recognizable, having been so ruthlessly tortured and scalped but Arnette knew who they were.

"It's Lars Sengstock and his son, Oliver," he sadly told the soldier. "I don't think they have kin around here. But they lived here for quite a while. You can leave them. We'll see to the burial. Was there a woman with them? A girl? I know that guitar. That belonged to a girl used to work here with these two men. Jesse Taylor, she was. Saloon people they all were. I kicked them out of town a while back. Too much trouble happening in the tavern. Never thought they'd end up like this, though. I'm feeling real bad about it."

"You weren't the one that did them in, Sheriff. Don't take this on yourself. Murdering varmints are to blame here. Not you, in the least. No woman anywhere around when we found them. Horses gone. Found no guns. Indian raid I'd guess, what with them being tortured with fire. Scalped and all. Can we leave them with you then?"

"Yeah. That'll be fine. Can your men carry them into the jail? I'll keep them there, until I can scare up a burying crew."

"Private Williams, Corporal Halstead. Get these bodies into the jailhouse. One more thing, Sheriff. Can you tell me where the Broken Spur Ranch is located? We got a report of some Indian activity on that property a week or so ago, and I wanted to see if there was information out there that could be of help."

"Just take this street to the west end of town, then go south. Six miles about. When you get there, look up a young fellow called Justin. Justin Trav. Tell him about the Sengstocks. Could you please see that he gets this guitar? He'll know whose it is."

As Tom Arnette watched the cavalry squad depart the town of Travis heading west on Pamela Street, he sat down on the wooden sidewalk in front of his office. He folded his hands, closed his eyes and, holding back tears, he began to pray.

"Dear God," he said. "Help me understand your plan. What is it you wish for me to do? Please, take this bitter cup from the lips of the people of Travis, Lord. Protect them from the lobo menace. They are your people, as I am your servant. Amen."

Reuben Pritchard had been a doctor for more than thirty years and never once had encountered a wound as disfiguring as the facial wound suffered by Pamela Trav. He carefully studied his sleeping patient. Filled with laudanum for pain and sleep, Pamela was in her fifth day since the injury. Searching for signs of healing or proud flesh, Doctor Pritchard ran his forefinger along the line of the wound.

His gentle touch awakened her. Her left eye opened fully, causing the bloodshot right eye—only a third opened—to assume a somewhat chilling presence in comparison. Pamela, only slightly awake, saw that the doctor's eyes were filled to overflowing.

"Is it as bad as all that?" Pamela hoarsely managed.

"It's my best work, Pamela. Still ain't very good. If you'd been in a big town you could've got a better doctor than me. I'm used to sewin' up horn-hooked cowhands, mule bites and such. I'm a poor choice for pretty faces like yours."

"Hand me my looking glass, Reuben. That hand mirror on the dresser there."

Reuben Pritchard had been through a lot of hard times during his life as a frontier doctor. He thought by now he was hardened enough to handle anything. Yet, as he handed over the glass to Pamela, he noticed his hand was shaking. Pamela studied her reflection in the glass a long time. The doctor noted a single tear rolled from her weak eye and trailed a little rivulet, as it followed along the edge of the inflamed scar.

"I'm so sorry, Pam. It breaks my heart I couldn't do better." Reuben put his face in his hands.

"Reuben, you're our doctor." Pamela sat as upright as she was able. "I wouldn't want nobody else." She wiped the tear away and changed the subject. "How's Colin? I've been so fretful about him."

"Well, that's some good news for you. Colin and Walter are both doing pretty good. Walter's fussin' about stayin' in bed, but I'm keeping him there until his blood pressure gets up a little higher. He just about bled out, you know. Colin's out of bed. Got him in a wheelchair."

"Wheelchair? Where did we get a wheelchair?"

"My office. I've had the thing for a long time. Never needed it till now. Colin hates it. He'd be walking around all over the place if I'd let him."

"I'm so glad he's up. Walter too. See Reuben, you're just the doctor this outfit needs." Pamela grew thoughtful. "Has he seen me yet? Does he know what I look like?"

"No, not yet. Oh, you can be sure he's tried to. He's been after me every day to bring him in here. I just wasn't sure the time was right yet. Since you're awake—how about if we bring him in now? I know he's dying to be with you."

"Oh Reuben, are you sure? What if he hates the way I look? Do you think he would still—would he still—" Her voice trailed off. She looked toward the window at a little sunbeam peeking through the partially draped opening.

"I'm lost here, Pamela. Who are we talking about? I thought we were talking about Colin Trav. You know—that cowboy you're married to. The Colin I know is going to be busting with pride in a wife that can do what you did."

"I didn't do much. They got away with Little Buck. He's our son, Reuben. How's Colin going to feel about that? About this face? This scar? My son? Our son?"

"Scar? Do you mean that badge of honor? I've known Colin a long time, Pam. I don't think he'd trade you. Not even for a speckled belly pup."

172

Chapter Eighteen

Robert Trav's assessment that the two lobos would not hide together proved to be wrong. Garcia had slipped down the slope a hundred and fifty yards when he spotted a slight movement within some high sawgrass at the edge of a pothole pond. Carefully studying the area, he at last was able to discern the distinct shapes of the pair.

Garcia settled himself down and kept them under surveillance. Almost as an afterthought, as he studied the terrain, he spotted a tiny flash of white fifty yards off to the right of the hidden pair.

Careful study on Garcia's part revealed he was looking at the boy, Buck. Still in his white night shirt, he was solidly bound to a tree. At that moment Garcia became aware of his horse, Diablo, moving down the hill and approaching the stray horse at the side of the dead Grey Wolf.

"Look, Michael. It is the horse of the Mexican, the pinto. He is loose! Might be that our pursuers are in trouble. No one would want to be afoot in this country." Red Stick was excited.

Michael added, "We should work up the slope. Not together. I'll take the right side. You slip around on the left. If we can catch them off guard, we can kill them both."

"But, you said we should kill only one. Leave one alive to tell of the ransom we want to return the boy."

"I've changed my mind." Michael stated. "These two are better trackers than I thought two old dull knives could be. They are more dangerous than I thought. We can kill them both and I'll approach the ranch with a white flag. You can keep the boy out of sight with you until I bring the money. Then we loose the boy to find his way home while we are far away. Or better. We can keep the boy. We sell him again another time. Also, they will not fight with us, when we have the boy."

Red Stick grunted his agreement. *He is right. Michael is the smartest of my band.*

"Let us start now," Michael spoke in a low voice. "But first let's see to the boy. He must not slip the cords."

Michael stepped a few feet near the body of the dead warrior Grey Wolf and caught the bridle of Garcia's Diablo. Leading the horse, he and Red Stick crept slowly back to the tree where Buck was tied.

At the same time, from a different direction, Garcia worked his way through the thicket, totally unseen until he was a scant forty yards from the prisoner. He stayed low in the brush but checked the chamber of the Winchester. He started to let the hammer of the gun ride in the safety notch, but as an afterthought he left the rifle fully cocked and kept his finger on the trigger.

Now the lobos approached the bound boy. Red Stick heartily tugged at the cords securing the boy's wrists, causing Buck to cry out a bit. At that moment, Garcia stood. Red Stick and Michael had their backs to him, but Buck's eyes widened, and his jaw dropped as he saw Juan Garcia plainly.

"Shoot 'em, Mister Garcia! Kill 'em both! Shoot!"

Red Stick and Michael wheeled in their tracks to see who the boy was calling to. They spotted Garcia at the same time. They wheeled and tried to run, but it was too late. Garcia's rifle barked, and the .44 took Red Stick right in the center of his back disabling him instantly.

As Red Stick crumpled to the ground, Michael tried to mount Garcia's Diablo. A sharp whistle from Garcia and the loyal pinto reared and wheeled on his rear hoofs at the same time. The result was he cleanly jerked away from a totally surprised Michael. Just as Garcia closed the chamber of the rifle on a new shell, Michael ducked behind the dead warrior's black horse and sprinted for the brushy thicket where he had concealed his own steed.

A blistering slug from Garcia's gun cut through the muscle of Michael's neck to his shoulder. Quickly working the lever of the rifle, Garcia let out two more shots at the fleeing Michael, who stumbled a bit, but continued his desperate course.

Michael was in the thicket and on his horse. In an instant he was racing headlong through the branches of the copse. Garcia whistled again and Diablo ran to his side. Garcia swung into the saddle and was prepared to head after the fleeing Michael when he heard the pleading of Little Buck.

"Please help me, Mister Garcia. Please, Juan—untie me."

Reluctantly, Garcia abandoned the chase. He felt more than one bullet had struck its mark and he reasoned the boy had been through enough. He went straight away to Little Buck and with his pocketknife began to work on his bonds. Almost at the same moment he freed the lad, they were joined by a panting Robert.

"Heard them shots and I came arunnin'. How's my boy? How are we a doin', Little Buck?"

"I'm fine, Papaw. Mister Garcia, he shot 'em up good."

"You came running, Patron? Why did you not ride your horse Punkin?"

Robert was puzzled for a moment.

"Damn, I forgot my horse. I hope he's still there."

It was then that they heard a groan from the fallen Red Stick.

"Reckon this here one's still alive," Robert spoke. "Johnny, take Little Buck back up the hill—see can you find my horse. I'll handle things here."

Garcia knew what Robert meant. Some things the boy was too young to see. Taking Little Buck in his arms, they mounted the pinto and rode back up the slope. Red Stick, with some of his last energy, had rolled onto his back. His head was propped against the very tree he had tied the boy to. Frothy blood was seeping from his nose and mouth.

Having spent a large part of his life among Indians, Robert Trav knew there was nothing the red man loathed so much as to be ridiculed. He knew Red Stick would soon be dead and he intended to upbraid him as much as he was able in the time that was left. Cruelty was not usually a part of his person. But this was the invader of his family. Lobo.

"Lookin' at all them bubbles," Robert was smiling, "I'd say you caught that one right in the lungs. Damn, I expect that hurts a might, don't it. 'Specially when you try to breathe. I had really hoped when we caught up with you that you wouldn'ta had to be shot. We'd of had us a white man's hangin'. Not much left of you to hang now. Wonder if you'll be dead afore the coyotes come? Hungry all the time, ain't they? I just want you to know that as soon as you're dead, I'm fixin' to scalp you. You know, same as you did all them other poor fellows.

"I would scalp you alive." Red Stick managed through a mouth filled with foamy blood, eyes burning with hate.

"Oh, I would you too, if you was a man," Old Robert taunted. "See, I'm a man and I could handle that. Big difference twixt you and me. When I walk, I make big thunder. When I fights, I fight real men and bears and catamounts and such. You—you must be some warrior's little sister. You make war on women and little boys. Was I to scalp you alive, you'd cry like a little papoose. Wet your britches too, I reckon. I'm gonna hang your scalp on a tree limb somewhere, so the crows can have it. All the scalps I have are the scalps of true warriors. I would be disgraced were I to keep some of your hair. Cowards make war on little boys. You got yourself a woman? A *walpu?* You are surprised I know some Comanche? Walpu? You have a good walpu?"

"Shlola," Red Stick managed. "Walpu is Shlola."

Robert thought for a few moments.

"Shlola. That's swan, right? Your woman is called after the swan. Damn, I'll bet she's pretty. Too bad you ain't never gonna see her no more. Don't you worry none though. If she's pretty enough she'll get herself another buck pretty soon. Not a lobo that chops up women's faces. Mayhaps she gets herself a real man now. Not a coward like you."

"Red Stick is last fighter of clan," he managed. His eyes fluttered back into his head and for a brief instant he thought of his father.

Then, as he died, "No Red Stick—I am *Baton Rouge.*"

*   *   *

Within an hour Robert and Garcia had fed Little Buck from their supplies. Garcia caught Red Stick's horse for the boy. A three-quarter moon was just rising. After they had salvaged the outlaws' guns and tack, they determined there was moonlight enough for night riding.

Bobwhite quail had just begun their little two-note whistle meant to bring their covey together as two weary old frontiersmen and a grateful, sleepy little boy commenced the long miles for home.

Chapter Nineteen

"So, you see, Lisa. we could really use your help. Mister Colin's finally up and usin' a wheelchair, but Miss Pamela still suffering somethin' jest terrible, an' it's been a few days now since them Indians did her so bad... That Comanche axe cleaved her right in the face. Ain't just that it's a terrible wound, but there's somthin' else too."

Bobby Baxter was soliciting Lisa to come to the Broken Spur to help with the nursing of the wounded.

"The whole thing sounds just terrible. What else is there?" Lisa asked.

"Well, I don't rightly know just how to say it. See— she's just awfully—well, she's—she's pretty ugly right now. I'm thinkin' she's sadder maybe than she is hurt. Maybe the hurt's more in her heart than it is in her face. Now it ain't like she's a vain woman or nothin' like that. There just ain't anybody more sweeter than Miss Pamela, but this here wound— well, it's pretty terrible. Doc Pritchard says she just cries when she sees herself in the lookin' glass. He took all the mirrors out of her room, just so she didn't go to lookin' to herself."

"Do you really think I could help her, Bobby?"

"She needs someone to talk with. Someone asides cowboys and horse wranglers. Someone like you who can tell her she's still pretty and, when that scar dries up, it ain't gonna be too bad."

179

"What about her husband?" Lisa wanted to know.

"'Course he tells her all kinds of good stuff, but she thinks he's tellin' her that on account of he's her husband and he's supposed to talk that way to her."

"Of course, I'll come, Bobby, if you think I can help. There's nothing going on at the Staghorn. Since Burton Cole and Winton Pollard took over, no one goes there anymore. The place is dirty. You can't even see out of the windows. They're drinking more than they're selling. They do owe me a little money, though. I need to pack up some things to last till you bring me back. I need a little break from that place. I just can't get Lars and Ollie off my mind anyway. So terrible."

"What if I wasn't thinkin' 'bout bringin' you back?"

"What are you talking about, Bobby? What are you saying?"

"Well, I was just thinkin'. You know—thinkin'—well, I was wonderin' if maybe, you and me, could kind of... Well, you know. Sort of be a couple?"

"Well for Christ's sake, Bobby Baxter! You and me been a couple since the first day I laid eyes on you! We've been goin' to get married ever since you and Justin raced the stagecoach that I was on into town. Be a couple, indeed! I ought to punch you! But, I live in those rooms above the Staghorn. I got stuff I need to fetch for a stay at the ranch, however long it might be."

"I never told you about it," Bobby said, "but see, I'm kind of top hand out to the Spur. Well, of course Old Mister Robert, he's my boss. I guess Mister Garcia's my boss too. And of course, Mister Colin—And Miss Pamela. I guess Justin's sort of my boss, too. Anyway, I fit in there somewhere.

"What I'm sayin' is, I'm entitled to live in one of the houses on the ranch. There's three or four houses out there. I can have one, if I want. I never did, 'cause I liked the bunkhouse and bein' with the boys. But anyway, there's a nice little house some settlers built on a hill overlookin' the Canadian. They didn't stay—had California fever, I think. Left this nice place with a barn, chicken shed and all. I can have it. I mean, you and me can have it. I mean *we* can have it, if you want to. We could marry—have the house. You wouldn't need the Staghorn no more. There's room in the big house for you till we can get settled in. I can't talk no more, Lisa. My throat is all dried out."

"You don't need to talk no more, Bobby. My ears are all dried out, too. Let's think on this a little bit. Meanwhile, I will come and stay with Pamela. Can you come after me, day after tomorrow? I want to get some things together and collect my thirty dollars Burton owes me."

"You don't need no money, Lisa. I got money for us. I get a cut of the herd sale, when I drive 'em to Dodge."

"Day after tomorrow." Lisa was sweet, but firm.

"Day after tomorrow," Bobby unenthusiastically agreed.

Colin Trav had maneuvered his wheelchair onto the front porch of the big house. He sat quietly, enjoying the afternoon sun. At his leisure he was slowly sipping at a two-ounce gill of good whiskey pilfered from Old Robert's personal stock.

His wound was neatly healing, although at times a deep breath could bring about an unrelenting pain. It was now the sixth day since the shooting, and it appeared he'd be in the wheelchair for many more days. Though Pamela was still hiding in her room most of the time and Robert and Garcia were out on the trail searching for Little Buck, a few things had improved recently, though it was still dark times in general for the Broken Spur.

Walter was back to part time cooking meals for the big house, as well as for the working hands, except now the widow of Old Wetherspoon had been assigned to helping him. Granny Wetherspoon was a stout woman in her sixties. Her broad, dark brown face was given to ready smiles. As her husband Amon, she had too been a slave. While he had been set free by the will of Henry Clay in 1850, she was not freed until Lincoln's Emancipation Proclamation of 1863.

No one knew how or when they had met, or if they were truly married. They had taken up housekeeping in one of the small cabins near the Broken Spur's high meadow. No one had ever said a harsh word about the pair. They worked hard, tended their own affairs and watched after the cherished little herd of the historic Longhorns stashed nearby.

Distraught by the murder of her husband, she was afraid she might be asked to leave the ranch now that Amon was gone. Instead, Pamela had assured her she was welcome on the Spur and could have the little cabin as long as she wanted it.

She could pick up her husband's wages if she would help out in the kitchen and care for the chickens. As it came to pass, she was an excellent cook and baker as well. She and Walter worked exceedingly well together.

"They were laughing so much, I thought they were drunk," Pamela told Colin.

"Were they?" Colin asked.

"No. They were making cornbread."

"Cornbread all that much fun, is it?"

"I think you had to be there."

Colin was enjoying these thoughts, when his dreamy demeanor was interrupted by Long John Barlow's greeting.

"Afternoon, Mister Colin." Long John approached the porch, battered Stetson hat in hand. "I was wonderin' if you might have a minute or two I could talk with you?"

"Well dang it all, Long John. How did you know I was just hankerin' for somebody to palaver with a bit. Pull one of them rockers over and sit with me." Then, raising the glass, "Would you care for a taste?"

"Thank you, no. I really don't want to take that much of your time, Mister Colin—I was just wonderin' if you'd heard much about the Staghorn lately?"

"Well, what I hear ain't too good. Bobby tells me Pollard and Cole kind of letting the place get run down. You know, we've had our hands full around here what with me gettin' shot—Miss Pamela and all. I've been meaning to look into the Horn, just haven't really had the time. Bobby says it's a mess down there, though. Why you askin' about it?"

"I never told nobody and I don't know hardly how to come at you about this… but, I been thinkin' a lot lately. Thinkin' about how I'd love to have me a saloon."

"Are you just jokin', Long John? Hell man, you're one of the best cowmen in this whole country. Horses too."

"I ain't sure I'm all that good. Thank you for thinkin' it, though." Long John was struggling. "Thing is though, I'm fifty-three years old come spring. I been pokin' cows a little more'n forty years. You know how it is, Mister

Trav. I been outdoors almost all of that forty. Feedin' and packin' hay in the winter. Roundup in spring. Then again in summer. Trail drive summer and fall. Just an old Stetson for a roof. I been thinkin' a lot about livin' indoors for a while. Sleepin' in a bed. Workin' under a real honest-to-God roof for a change. Swappin' stories with old saddle pals. Broken Spur's been mighty good to me for a long time now, Mister Trav. I'd never just quit on you. I always figured I'd probably die here and be in Mister Robert's little cemetery someday. But—well, was I to see you owned a horse that wasn't bein' treated right, I'd take care of that for you. Was somebody a stealin' from you, I'd take care of that, too. Things at the Horn are bad. Real bad. I know you still own it, although Winton Pollard tells everybody it's his. I'm ready for an indoor job and you got a place needs cleanin' up. I'm wondering if we can work somethin' out."

"I guess Winton Pollard ain't worth much, huh?" Colin was in thought.

"I don't usually run nobody down, Mister Trav, but them two—Burton Cole and Winton Pollard—they're like tits on a boar. Worthless"

"To tell you the truth," Colin responded. "Until Papa Robert and Garcia gets back, and I find out how my son is, I don't really care much about the bar—anything else for that matter. You've been a cowman a long time. Are you for sure you want to run a bar, John?"

"I'm for sure I'd like to try it."

Colin's mind was already made up and he needed no time to think it over.

"Is the pay you're getting as a cowhand alright, until you get the place running again?"

"More than fair."

"When do you want to do this?"

"What about today?" Long John asked.

Colin sipped at the fine bourbon. After a short pause he said, "Tell Pollard and Cole that I'm turning the place over to you, Long John. If they have trouble understanding that, you tell them to see me about it. Any trouble with them, Sheriff Arnette's pretty close by. If you're sure you want to do this, go ahead. Only condition is Old Robert needs to approve it. I don't see that as a problem, but after all, the Staghorn belongs to him."

The two shook hands and Colin watched Long John stride to the corral where he caught a horse. He saddled, bridled and was on the road to town in less than twenty minutes.

Broken Spur is losin' one hell of a cowboy today, Colin thought.

"Riders a comin'! Riders! Mister Robert—Mister Garcia!" Wind Walker was running hard around the house to the front porch. He had spotted the trio coming up the trail from the south. No one had seen Wind Walker this excited before. He was literally beside himself. "They bringin' Little Buck! Old Robert and Mister Garcia—they done saved our Little Buckaroo!"

Wind Walker's proclamation soon brought all the Spur hands that were in the area together on the front lawn of the big house. All were shaking hands, slapping backs and the scene was one of loving chaos. The old hunters were home and the beloved small captive had been rescued. Little Buck was hugged, patted, and had his hair tousled over and over.

It would be Bobby Baxter that noticed Old Robert's unusual appearance. He sidled up to Justin and asked, "Why is your papaw wearing that little girly skirt?"

"I don't know, Bobby. Why don't you go over and ask him?"

The expression on Justin's face was a sly one of warning. Baxter thought for a few sparse moments and replied.

"I think I'll just let it go."

Chapter Twenty

Michael pushed his stolen horse as hard as he was able. Crashing through the brush, he was trying to make himself invisible to Garcia's rifle. The tendon from his right shoulder to the base of his neck burned with the fire that can only come from near molten lead.

After a twenty-minute run, shock overtook him, and he slipped from the saddle of the galloping horse and fell to the ground. Though he was awake and alert, he found he was unable to move. He lay still, covered by the tall grass as he heard his horse sprint away from him and out of earshot. Now his stolen horse was gone. The Winchester resting in the saddle scabbard was gone as well.

Very slowly his mobility began to return. Even so, he lay still on the ground and listened for the rider he was certain was searching for him. He finally determined after a thirty-minute wait that he was not being pursued. Indeed, there was no rider searching the high brush and chaparral for him.

They think I'm dead, he reasoned. *Gonna be dark soon. I'm just going to lay myself here till good and dark. Maybe I can catch my horse. Can steal another one, I guess. Bet that Mexican thinks he hit me with more than one shot. Luck, I guess. Lot luckier than Red Stick.* Michael lay back on the earth. He believed he could rest an hour or maybe two, as he waited for it to get dark enough to move about in safety. He was not sure that Garcia wasn't still in the area, maybe still looking.

After an hour of rest, Michael was back on his feet. As he moved through the thicket, he stopped often to listen.

Could it be? He pondered. The Mexican had given up the search without looking for his dead body? Now he was near another large pothole. Still just light enough to see, he found he was near willows. With his knife he scraped a handful of green bark from a small sapling. His people had chewed the bark of the willow for centuries as a pain reliever.

Jimson weed was far better, but in this area was always more difficult to find. He knew the willow would not completely erase the pain from Garcia's gunshot, but it would ease it somewhat. It would make it easier to travel. Some of the elements that made up willow sap and bark in more civilized regions of the world were already recognized as key ingredients for the manufacturing of aspirin. A pain killer.

The bleeding had stopped on its own. He would need to take care and not disturb the sealing clot. Michael really had only a scant idea of where he was as he forced his way through heavy brush. He was familiar, at least, with general directions and he felt certain he was headed north.

With the stars at night, he could correct his path and compensate for any variance in his daylight travel. He elected to stay within heavy cover, though. He was not up for a fight just yet. After three days of pushing through wilderness, he sensed the brush was giving way in front of him. He was approaching some type of a clearing. Now on hands and knees, he crawled forward to investigate whatever he might be approaching.

It was a homesite. A lovely two-story house of clapboard and fieldstone. Surrounded by flowers, trees, and plantings, the scene was a tranquil one. The place had a smallish barn just large enough for buggy stock and a milk cow. His investigation determined he had come upon an abandoned homestead.

A deserted and overgrown backyard garden had become the feeding ground of the local deer herd. Wild razorbacks and armadillo had rooted here, too. The place was deserted, but it had not been so for very long. This homesite would prove to be the parsonage of the Travis Trinity Lutheran Church. Deserted only recently, as the Pastor Marcus Armstrong and new bride, blacksmith Andrew Caldwell's widowed sister-in-law, Morgana, went to investigate Morgana's holdings in Indiana.

Michael wasted no time breaking in once he had determined the place was truly empty. Of course, his first search would be for any food that the former residents had left behind. He certainly did not find much. A half-gallon of sorghum molasses and a mold-covered block of cheese were the total results of his search.

Once he had scraped the mold from the cheese, he thought it tasted just fine. Sorghum molasses though, he consigned to the taste preference of white men. He tried spreading some on the cheese, but found the cheese was better without it. It was in the small barn that he found the sack of parched corn and the wooden crate filled with apples. These revived him quickly. Imagine his delight at finding the forgotten quart bottle of whiskey secreted within the roof rafters.

Within a day he had waylaid one of the smallest of the razorback hogs and had killed it with his knife secured to a mop handle and used as a spear. He felt safe at using the kitchen stove to cook up pieces of the small swine, reasoning no one would see the chimney smoke after dark.

Michael soon learned he was only fifty or sixty yards from the east end of Pamela Street, the dusty thoroughfare that led to the west, right through the town of Travis. After dark he would creep out into the yard. From there he could have an undetected view of what little nighttime activity took place on east end of the town's fronting street.

He was looking almost directly at the east wall of the Staghorn Saloon. On two occasions he had viewed a young woman climbing the stairway attached to the wall that led to the rooms above the saloon. He knew she was young by the way she sometimes took the steps two at a time. Always within minutes after she reached the top and entered into the rooms, a small light would appear.

It is a small lamp. Perhaps a candle, he thought. *She must work in that saloon. I wonder how much money she has.*

He vowed he would soon know.

With the three-quarter moon through about half of its nightly arc, Michael estimated it must be close to midnight. It had been more than an hour since he had observed the young woman exit the Staghorn Saloon and make the climb of the stairway to her rooms above. The dim glow of an oil lamp had burned steadily from her window since her entry.

He had hoped to attack her when she had gone to bed and was muddled with sleep. He could not know that she was up very late only because she was busily packing up her belongings in readiness for her move to the big house at the Broken Spur.

The moonlight cast a smoky glow over the community corral located to the rear of the Staghorn. Michael had earlier stolen and made ready the horse he wanted for his escape. A sorrel gelding now stood saddled, bridled, and tied to the hitch ring on the gate of the corral.

From hiding, Michael had carefully studied the eight or nine mounts within the pen. Selecting able horseflesh was as normal to a Comanche as a heartbeat. Michael had wanted a horse that looked as though he could run. Lean without being thin. Tall, but with strong forelegs and fetlocks. Large, stout knees. A smooth, broad rump, but without a fat coating. A sculpted neck. All of this and an intelligent face with foxy, perky ears facing forward in a constant state of alert. Of course, he carefully investigated all four feet. He determined the sorrel gelding was well shod. He felt confident he had selected the toughest and fastest horse from the little herd.

For a moment Michael gave thought to what he was doing. Why was he planning this attack at all? It was true the lone woman might have food and money he could certainly use. Maybe even a gun. But in a moment of self-honesty, he admitted to himself it was a matter of revenge. Burning hate.

The Broken Spur raid had been a total disaster. Three lobos dead. Their captive, rescued. The entire, carefully planned attack ended in humiliation. The thought of two old men far past their prime reversing the intended ambush upon himself and Red Stick anguished Michael.

Perhaps he could redeem himself as a terrorist by a ruthless murder attack on a lone woman. He would leave her dead and the saloon in flames. Conceivably, he thought he could reignite the terror the four lobos had originally intended to visit upon these invading whites.

As silent as death, Michael climbed the stairs.

Inside her rooms Lisa was busily packing her carpet bag. She was glad to be leaving these rooms as well as the saloon and the life that went with it. Her love for Bobby Baxter was on her mind and she felt as happy as she ever remembered being. Then, she heard that distinct squeak of the third stair tread from the top,

It's Jesse! she thought. *She's come back!*

Lisa ran to the door and threw it open expecting to find her best friend. Instead, she was now face to face with a half-naked stranger, a large skinning knife in his right hand. Before she could speak, the stranger stuck her full in the face with his left fist, driving her back into the room. He was upon her at once.

Pushed back farther into the room, she retreated until, at last, she felt the back of her knees come in contact with the edge of Jesse's bed. As she collapsed, falling backwards onto the bed, the intruder leaped astride her brandishing his knife. Lisa cried out and, with both hands, tried to fend off the slashing blade.

Koiniata, Michael thought. The Comanche word for rape. *No need to lose this chance.* He longed to see her breasts. Using the knife, he cut through the neck cord of her blouse. As he was parting the cloth of her shirt in a last effort to protect her modesty Lisa tried mightily to buck her attacker from her chest.

He struck her with another violent blow causing her to roll a bit to the side. Her right arm somehow slipped under Jesse's pillow and her hand struck something hard. Hard and cold. For a moment she could not imagine what she was feeling. Then it struck her.

It's a gun! It's Jesse's little thirty-two. She must have forgotten it.

In an instant she had thumbed back the hammer and was pointing the gun squarely into Michael's face. At the sight of the pistol, Michael halted his attack and reared himself back still sitting on her torso. He instinctively knew the game was at a startling reversal.

She pushed the barrel against his chest. Gritting his teeth, clenching his eyes he steeled himself against the gunshot he knew was coming. She pressed the trigger. Expecting the explosion of the pistol, she readied herself.

There was no explosion. Just a sharp click of the hammer falling onto an empty chamber. Michael recovered himself quickly. In an instant he was again in command.

It's unloaded! he said to himself. Recovering now, he grinned evilly at Lisa and waved the knife at her throat. He ripped open her shirtfront. Using both hands, Lisa forced the pistol's hammer back for the second time. This time, when she pulled the trigger, the little gun exploded with an ear-splitting roar and a belch of white gun smoke.

How could this little gun be that loud? she thought.

The lead bullet sped its way through Michael's throat and lodged in the ceiling of the room. Excess black powder sparks filled the air surrounding his head and setting his long, loose locks of hair afire. At once more than a dozen flaming powder grains pocked his face.

Michael tried to rise, but as death overtook him, he collapsed, his full weight falling on top of Lisa.

Lisa, struggling mightily, was at last able to free herself of the weight of Michael's body by rolling him off of her and onto the floor. The next few minutes were a blur to her. Numb with shock and terror, her mind went blank. She felt the room was spinning out of control.

The stench of gun smoke and singed hair was sickening sweet. Bile rose in her throat and after a few seconds she vomited uncontrollably. Moments passed and at last she began to surface from her daze.

The first thing she was actually aware of was that she was cradled in the strong arms of Long John Barlow.

"Take it easy now, Missy," he cooed as if he were soothing an injured horse. He was adjusting the front of Lisa's blouse to restore her decorum and at the same time relieve his embarrassment of seeing her uncovered breasts.

"Jist be easy Miss Lisa. I'm gettin' you out of here. I'm takin' you to Bobby. You gonna be alright. I heerd that there gunshot and I knowed somthin' was wrong up here. I'll get you to Bobby. I'll take you out to the Spur. You'll be alright. You gonna be fine—You just let old Long John take some care of you now. I'll fetch us a buggy. You come right along now. It's all over. You did fine killin' that there no account lobo feller."

The reunion between Little Buck and his mother was a mixture of laughter and tears and more laughter and more tears. As their eyes met, Little Buck could only see the ghastly red and blue scar across Pamela's face left by the flying tomahawk of Red Stick.

The wound extended from the corner of her right eye down to the corner of her mouth. The stitches used to close the gaping cut was threatening and lent a macabre appearance to the vision. Pamela's right eye was totally inflamed and constantly leaked a stream of tears down her once lovely face. Little Buck buried his face against her breast to avoid seeing it.

Finally, as he came to grips with the mutilation's reality, he was able to share in the sheer revelry of being home, of being with his mother and father. At last, Pamela was so overcome with happiness and exhaustion that Colin felt it necessary to end the reunion and let her rest.

As Colin guided Little Buck from Pamela's bedroom, the boy suddenly buried his face in his father's chest and gave way to great sobs and flowing tears of sadness.

"What's wrong, son?" Colin wanted to know.

"It's that scar on her face," Little Buck cried. "It's all my fault."

"Why in the world would you ever think that was your fault, son?"

"'Cause those men came to get *me*. If it wasn't for *me*, she'd be alright."

"Those men were foul, no account horse dung, son. Nothing they did should you ever take the blame for. Not one thing. Anyway, they're dead now. They have paid the price for coming after you. Your mom is going to be fine. Sometimes it just takes a little time for things to work out."

"But that big cut—It's so terrible, Papa. So—so ugly." Colin pulled the youngster close to him and enfolded him in his arms. The boy buried his face in Colin's collar attempting to hide his tears.

"Try to look at it like this son—that scar –that scar is like a medal soldiers get when they do something special. Something brave. When I look at your mother's face, I see something fearless, something perfect. Your momma stood up to danger. She was ready to die to save us all. That's pretty special, son. You should try to remember that. The one other thing to always remember is that those men won't be able to cause any trouble for anyone again. Grandpa Robert and old Garcia did away with them."

"I'm glad they're dead, Papa. Papaw Robert says there's some men just ain't fit to live."

"And that's the truth, son. That's the God's truth."

Curiously, both Colin and Walter Beasley were injured in the Red Stick raid far more seriously than Pamela. However, they were both up and about their business within just a few days, though Colin still used the wheelchair occasionally and Walter had help in the kitchen. Pamela, though, was still bedfast a great portion of the time and being daily attended by Lisa and Doctor Pritchard.

The addition of Lisa Strong to the care of Pamela Trav had proven to be a good one. Attentive and truly caring, she was leading Pamela toward a certain recovery.

Colin noted that Pamela cried a lot more than he had ever seen before. Sometimes she would lie silent in her bed and stare at the ceiling for hours at a time. It seemed a great, mysterious melancholia had settled upon her. Her demeanor perplexed and saddened Colin. Her once clear and decisive manner had given way to a morose personality ever so peculiar.

Justin also did all he could to cheer his mother. He read to her daily from the family Bible. This was something she had always dearly loved in the past. Now, he was never sure whether or not she really heard him.

"That's just beautiful," she would say to him. Her voice, though, was distant and expressionless. Her eyes fixed upon the ceiling.

"It's like a fine horse with a broken spirit," Doctor Pritchard had explained to Colin. "Sometimes they recover from it, sometimes not. My daddy had a horse like that once. He bought it from the widow of a Texas Ranger—got himself killed somehow. Left his horse behind. Anyway—brought the horse home. He wouldn't eat. Wouldn't drink. Just got worse off every day. Missing his old master, I'd think. My kid brother had this old blue tick hound named Lightning. For some reason this dog got to visiting with this horse 'bout every day. At first they're just smellin' each other's noses. Pretty soon, though, they're chasing each other around the corral. Just playing like a couple of kids. Well, horse, he turned out to be a good one. Matter of fact, that's the horse I came to Travis on back in '74. I'd say that dog was to my horse what Lisa Strong is to your wife, Colin. When I'm around her, she sure don't talk much. Around Lisa though, she's a chatterbox. Laughs a lot too. They talk about dresses. Fixing hair. Woman stuff. I'd bet on Pamela coming back to herself though, Colin. She's as tough as they come. Matter of fact, I think more than worrying about her wound, she's a mite more upset about not killing the son of a bitch that threw that hatchet at her."

CHAPTER TWENTY-ONE
Summer 1889

"I have something you need to see." Lisa offered the brown paper envelope to Bobby Baxter.

"A letter? Who sent you a letter, Lisa?"

"It was waiting for me at the sheriff's office. Sheriff Tom said the Wells Fargo stage left it there last Wednesday. It nearly caused me to faint when I read it. It's from Jesse."

"Jesse!" Bobby was stunned. It had been nearly a year since Jesse Taylor had boarded an eastbound Wells Fargo coach and disappeared from the town of Travis, presumably forever. Most of the citizenry of Travis promptly forgot all about her. But, not all. She had been Lisa Strong's closest friend.

Bobby Baxter recalled with great delight the Sundays he and Justin had picnicked with Lisa and Jesse. Indeed, Bobby and Lisa had the most pleasant of memories of the lithe, fair-haired Jesse.

For Justin Carstin though, the recollections were of a very different nature. No day passed without Justin longing for the company of Jesse Taylor. He thought of her as he went about his job among the cattle and as well when he bunked at night. He thought about her safety. He questioned where she could be.

At times he brooded deeply. He wondered how he had lost her, how he could have let her get away from him.

"What's it say?" Bobby wanted to know about the letter. "Where is she? She okay?"

"Do you want to read it?"

"No. That would take too long. Just tell me about it."

"She's in a place called Arrowhead," Lisa went on.

"I know Arrowhead," Bobby exclaimed. "It's a ways east of here. Almost to the Arkansas. What's she about there?"

"Says she's working in a shop that makes dresses."

"Jesse? A dressmaker?" Bobby sounded incredulous.

"That's what it says. She says she's through with saloons and taverns forever."

"Dang! Hard to believe," Bobby responded. "What else does she say?"

"She asks that I don't tell Justin where she is."

"Are you really not going to tell Justin? Are you not tellin' him, even though you know how troubled he is about not knowin' where she is? If she's even alive?"

"She asked *me* not to tell him. She didn't say that *you* should not tell him."

Taking the letter from Lisa's hand, Bobby was off to search the ranch and to find his friend, Justin.

"Momma." Justin began. Within an hour after Justin had read Jesse's letter a family meeting had been called. Pamela, Colin, Old Robert and Juan Garcia sat looking one to the other in the living room of the big house. Lisa and Bobby Baxter had been included.

"Momma, she's alive!" Justin began. "She's in a place that Bobby knows. Place called Arrowhead. In the Indian nation, I think. Near the Arkansas."

"I know Arrowhead." Colin added. "'Bout a hundred and fifty miles straight down the Canadian. It's a Quaker town."

"Quaker?" Justin asked.

"Good folks. Different though. Milk cows. Make cheese. Raise hogs and chickens. Ride about everywhere in buggies with good horses."

"Well, she's there. Makin' dresses. Momma, Colin —I got to go to her. Bring her back here."

A few tears were evident in Justin's eyes.

"Are you sure about this, son?" Old Robert asked. "You know she left without even a word to you. Why did she ever leave in the first place?"

"That's 'cause Oliver made her feel so bad about something that happened a long time ago. Something that don't matter a damn to me. I think she was afraid somebody might say somethin' to her about that. Hurt her more I'd guess. You know that ain't right. Nobody in Travis would dare say somethin' about her if I was there."

"You see Justin?" Lisa added. "That's what's wrong. She wasn't bothered about what anybody might say to her. She's thinking those things Oliver said *about* her. They might have got around. About how it might hurt you... Your family. She wouldn't want you hurt. Certainly, you'd defend her. She wouldn't want you to have to."

"God damn that Oliver!"

"Ease up on the language, son," said Colin. "This is your momma sittin' here."

"But don't you see, Colin. I've got to go to her. I have to see her in person. I have to ask her to come back here with me. I have to know how she feels. I can't lose her again. I don't even know what I'm going to say to her."

"Might tell her you love her." Colin remarked.

"Tell her Bobby and me are marrying pretty soon. I'd expect that to bring her about." Lisa chimed with an infectious grin.

"What if she won't come back with you?" Pamela asked. "What do you do then?"

"Then, I guess I'll stay with her. I guess—"

"What if I don't want you to go?" Old Robert asked.

"Well then, it'll be the only time in my life I ever disobeyed you."

"I see you have to go," said Colin. "Do you have money?"

"I'm fine that way."

"I will ride with you," Juan Garcia said, feeling that the need to protect Justin was up to him. "Together we will have a fine ride."

"No, Juan. This is something I must do alone. Thank you, but no."

"Ride if you must." Pamela's tears traced the scar left by Red Stick's tomahawk. "Remember, this is your home. We love you. If Jesse is to come back with you, we will love her."

Old Robert added the "Amen."

It was nearly eight o'clock the next morning when Justin had made all the preparations for the journey that awaited him. Bobby Baxter had told him to wait by the porch and he would bring his horse from the stable. Justin and Lisa, Colin and Pamela stood quietly waiting. Old Robert and Juan Garcia added to the gathering. All stood silent. Then instead of the mount Justin usually rode, he was more than a little surprised to see Bobby approaching him and leading Rocket.

"Why are you bringing me your horse, Bobby? You aren't goin'."

"It's going to be a long hard trip for you, Justin. I want you to have the best horse on the place. And here he is."

"Bobby, I can't take your horse. You and Rocket—Well there's no way. Just no way can I separate you two."

"Get on the horse, Justin. I want you to have him."

"Are you sure about this, Bobby?"

"Just get on the damn horse!" It was Lisa at the top of her voice. "Just get on the horse and leave! Go!"

Justin slipped his left foot into the stirrup and Rocket shied away.

"Don't fret," Bobby said. "He'll get used to you."

Rocket turned his face to Bobby as if to ask, "Are you sure this is alright?"

Bobby took the reins and held Rocket while Justin mounted. Bobby leaned forward. He rubbed his face on the cheeks of the stallion. He kissed the velvet nose.

"Be a good horse, Rocket. Take care of Justin for us. Bring him home if you can."

Justin turned Rocket toward the lane. The big roan started off with a soft trot and slowly slid into a gentle canter. Horse and rider were about to disappear from view when Pamela asked.

"I wonder if we'll ever see our boy again?"

Colin stepped of the porch and started walking to the barn. He turned his back and walked swiftly away to conceal the mist in his eyes. It was feeding time for the livestock.

"Hope so," he said. "Hope so."

Juan Garcia slapped his riding crop against his leg.

"Caramba!" Garcia nearly shouted. "That rider you see is Justin Carstin. Don't you know him? That is Justin Carstin! Don't you know he is top hand of the Broken Spur? Of course he'll be back. He'll bring his little filly back, too. Don't you fear for him. He is Justin Carstin. He is mi hombre!"

EPILOGUE
West Point, New York
Fall 1899

"I'll walk along with you," Captain Howard said. "I haven't been over there in a very long time. What paper are you a writer for—Is it Donald? You did say your name was Donald?"

The younger man nodded as he retrieved a small notebook from a coat pocket and wrote the captain's name. Donald Eastman was a thin, bookish type with black-rimmed eyeglasses that seemed ready to slip from his nose at any moment. He wore a tweed suit that was warm for the time of the year. Captain Howard noticed the cuffs displayed long, hard wear. He took an immediate liking to this studious young man.

"Captain Howard. Have I got that right?" Donald asked.

The captain, a stout man in his late sixties wore an old-fashioned heavy mustache and still looked formidable in his elegant union uniform.

"Yep. Alton Howard. Cleveland, Ohio. Been stationed here in West Point since the Red River war ended. More'n twenty-five years."

Donald Eastman scrawled something in the little notepad.

"Sounds like your retirement age, Captain Howard."

"Well past that son. Being forced into retirement next month. That don't mean I'm leaving here though. Goin' to stay right here on this West Point campus. I'll be a civilian employee, but I'll not leave the cemetery. You see, the residents hereabouts count on me."

It took a moment for the writer to see the intended humor in the remark.

"Aren't you anxious to go home, Captain? See the family? Old folks?"

"No family, young man. Never was but a few of us. Some died in the war. Rest scattered. Went west maybe. Lots of folks did that, you know. Especially the southerners. Some of them, even the poor ones, got so used to living that genteel southern style life they just couldn't bear seeing what happened to their beloved south. I can't say I blame them. Damned carpetbaggers and loan slickers. Usury and thieving everywhere. Chopping up the leftovers as it were. You didn't tell me what paper your with. Or did you? I can forget my own name seems like these days."

Eastman took his time with his explanation.

"No paper, sir. I'm a—I'm what you call a freelance writer. A month ago, I was on an Ohio riverboat near Louisville, Kentucky. Fellow got on and sat beside me out on the deck. We talked a lot. Well, I should say he talked a bit. He told me he was from El Paso, Texas and he had these stories about man named Mackenzie, Ranald Mackenzie. I just could not believe all the things he said about this man. Tell you the truth, I'd never heard of him. From what this Texan said he ought to be in the history books. So, I thought I'd look into it. See if there's a story here.

"Oh, my lord, son. There's more than just a story. There's a legend. A saga. A story? Ranald Mackenzie is a lot more than just a story. Greatest American hero I'd guess ever was. Ain't been dead long enough to be in a history book. He will be though. For sure."

Donald Eastman was puzzled.

"So why don't more people know about him?"

The captain fished a half-smoked cigar from his union blue jumper. He moistened the chewing end and lighted the stump with a blue tip match that he scratched on his belt buckle. The sun was high now. A slight breeze drifted in from the Hudson as they walked side by side toward an imposing stone fixture.

"Whatever you write, I'd like my name left out. I'll tell you about a truly great American, but then I'll have to tell you about a great U.S. Army coverup, too. If the army knew I was telling the tale—Well, it could be bad for me."

"I protect my sources, Captain. Let me in on the scuttlebutt. Not a word will ever be accredited to you."

"If you're sure about that we can start right here. See that giant stone finger pointing at the sky?" Captain Howard pointed to the huge cement-limestone obelisk that identified the West Point cemetery. "He's buried right alongside of that thing. My opinion is a flagpole would be better. But then nobody asked me. It is fitting he's buried here. He graduated the head of his class in 1862. Fought in damn near every Civil War battle. All the big ones, anyhow. Got himself all shot to hell and just never gave an inch."

Donald Eastman was caught up in curiosity.

"Battles? Anything I might have heard of?"

"Bull Run? Antietam? Gettysburg? How about Five Forks, Petersburgh?" The captain was rattling them off. Donald was astonished.

"Damn! You've about named the whole war. And he was wounded too?"

"Six times." The captain said. "Seven if you count the Comanche arrow he caught with his leg in the Red River fight."

Donald knew he was on the path to a remarkable story.

The old soldier added, "Seemed like every time he got hurt, he also got promoted. Grant, himself, promoted him all the way up to a brigadier. Three months later he's the youngest brevet major general ever in the American military service. That still holds by the way."

"What's brevet mean?" Donald wanted to know.

Captain Howard smiled broadly.

"Army secret. That's when you get the title but not the pay. All this fighting and him in command as a major general and he's still on lieutenant's wages. Anyway, when the Civil War ends General Grant gets himself elected President. Same time 'bout everyone wants to be moving into the west. Comanche, Sioux and Cheyenne and a few more Indian bunches I never heard of seems determined to keep the land they been on for a few centuries. There's the rub. Grant needs a fighting man, so he orders Mackenzie to Fort Richardson out in Jacksboro Texas. Now he's back to his permanent pay grade as a captain. He's put in charge of the 4th Cavalry. Ever hear about the 4th?"

Donald Eastman shook his head. Captain Howard answered emphatically.

"Buffalo soldiers. Negroes. No commander wanted anything to do with them. Turned out Mackenzie loved every mother's son of them and thy loved him right back. This was something Mackenzie didn't know beans about. During the war he wasn't popular with his men. His discipline was too tough, they all said. These black troopers got along with him just fine. I always wondered what was the difference. I'm ashamed to say it, but I think the blacks were just used to being treated poorly. The whites he had commanded had never been treated as harshly as the colored. That was 1871. The battle of North Fork. First time he met the Comanche in combat."

"North Fork?" Donald asked.

"North Fork of the Red River." Captain Howard answered. "Up near the panhandle. Two big leaders, chiefs I guess you could call them. Kal-Wotche and Mow-way had just been terrorizing the area. Killing small ranchers and farmers. Burning anything they couldn't carry away. Kidnapping women and some kiddies, too, I've been told. When Mackenzie hit them, it was called a massacre. Buffalo Soldiers wiped 'em out. Then there was the Red River war. About the same results. It was the Palo Duro Canyon fight that pretty much ended Comanche troubles though."

Donald responded. "I know about that one. That fellow on the river boat I told you I met. He said the soldiers found the central camp of the Comanche and raided them just at dawn. Caught them unaware and destroyed the entire camp. Tipis, weapons, food. All of it. But I just have to ask you—The part about the horses. Was that part of the story really true?"

"Well, to tell the truth, that part is the saddest and the truest. There were about three hundred warriors in that camp. Some say Quanah Parker of the Quahadi Comanche, and Kicking Bird of the Kiowa were together in that bunch.

Lone Wolf, Dull Knife. Regular roll call of all the big chiefs. Somehow, they vanished. One sergeant told me that the earth just swallowed them. Out of three hundred only seventeen warriors were killed. But Mackenzie destroyed all that they had left. Horses, too. He ordered his men to trap the Comanche horse herd in the Palo Duro canyon. At Mackenzie's command the troopers shot nearly one thousand and five hundred Comanche horses. Those dead horses lay spread out in the Texas sun and poisoned the air for weeks."

"Damn! So, it's true. It really happened!"

The captain nipped a bit of the cigar off and chewed it for a moment. He was somber.

"I was with him during this time. I was a second lieutenant assigned to horse care and procurement."

Donald thought he must be at the end of the story. He said, "I'd have to say that was a bang-up career."

"There's more, Donald," the captain continued. "If you're not in a hurry, I'll tell it to you. I like telling it. I was there. I saw it and lived with it. Would you like the rest of it?"

"My lord! How can there be more? Of course, I'd like to hear it. Hear it all. The coverup you mentioned earlier. I'd like to know whatever you can tell me about that."

The captain maneuvered Donald to one of the stone benches placed in the cemetery for those who needed a rest after the long hike. As they sat, Donald retrieved a pack of Picayune cigarettes from an inside jacket pocket. He lit one up with a kitchen-type match.

"A ready-made, huh?" Captain Howard asked. "Could I have one of those?"

The two sat in silence for a while. Then Captain Alton Howard resumed his tale.

210

"Mackenzie had always been a teetotaler. Never had a strong drink in his life, I'd imagine. That changed after Palo Duro and the horse killin'. He started visiting El Paso more and more. Well, part of that was his duty. There was a command post there he had to report too pretty often. There's a hotel there. It's a low place. Buffalo hunters. Indian traders. Some whores too. The upshot is he meets a lawyer he likes. Name was Tunstall. Got a big house so when Mac—I call him Mac sometimes. Well, he starts rooming with Tunstall when he has to go to El Paso. 'Nother reason he likes this arrangement is Tunstall's pretty young daughter, Miss Florida. She's a lot younger than Mackenzie but nonetheless things start to heat up betwixt them. Mac starts looking into retirement. He buys himself a ranch and all of us thinking we'll hear wedding bells soon.

"But, it don't happen. He don't retire and there's no wedding. He gets a new set of orders to help out with some Indian problems in Fort Sill, Oklahoma. He ups and leaves. Well, it gets to be a fairly long time, so Florida marries a doctor named Sharpe. In about a year they have a little boy. Sadly though, Doctor Sharpe dies in about two years. She and the little boy continue to live with Florida's father. Now out in Fort Sill, Mac's riding in a wagon. Something spooks the horses and he's pitched out of the wagon and squarely on his head."

"Did that kill him? Donald asked.

"No. But it might have been better for all if it had. He's somehow strange and different after that fall. Drinks more alcohol too. Comes back to El Paso and right away takes up with Florida again. This time a wedding is for sure. They exchange their vows on Christmas day. Now as strange as it seems, he disappears on their wedding night. Two days later someone finds him in an El Paso alley tied to a wagon wheel and beaten nearly to death."

"Oh, my God!" Donald chimed in. "What in the world could happen next?"

"Army surgeon tries to patch him and get him on his feet. But it just don't work. The doctors declare him insane. Not fit for duty. They retire him and commit him to a New York insane asylum." He paused here and was thoughtful for a long moment. "He has sister name of Harriet who tries to get him back on his feet, but it just cannot be. He died on January 19th of 1889. That's when the army buried him here. Florida never remarried is what I hear. For a while the army didn't feel good about his insanity. But his career was just so great they could not hide his light. That, friend Donald is the story. You reckon you could write it up?"

Donald drew heavily on his smoke.

"I'm not sure" he said. "I don't know if I'm a good enough writer to handle a story like that. I'm not sure anyone would believe it anyway. What could have ever been harsh enough to drive man that strong insane?"

"I've pondered that a lot. Was it the men he had killed? The battles he fought? His old wounds come to haunt him? Failure at loving a woman? Mostly, I've thought it might have something to with all those horses he killed at Palo Duro Canyon. You know cavalry men love horses above all. Else they wouldn't be cavalry."

Donald Eastman gazed at the upright stone. "Do you think he was insane when he had the horses shot?

"I think a better bet would be shooting the horses probably helped a lot in the losing of his mind."

The two men sat and smoked until the sun began to set. The captain felt good that he had told the story. Donald Eastman was glad he had heard it. Neither knew what they would do next.

ABOUT THE AUTHOR

Gary Harmon was born and raised in Evansville, Indiana. His father was a cattle dealer specializing in moving Texas calf crops to the feed lots of Indiana, Illinois and Kentucky. From this background it was natural for Gary to enter into meat packing and livestock trading on his own. He served as a buyer/seller of livestock in the markets of Evansville; Owensboro, Kentucky; Chicago, Illinois; and Kansas City, Missouri.

As a boy and young man, horses were of constant interest to Gary. When he was six, he was given a Shetland pony named Junebug. Many other horses would follow.

Spending his early life among livestock dealers and traders, he was to hear many tales of western derring-do. Some were true. Some were half true. Some were bald-faced lies. Gary thought them all wonderful.

A U.S. Army veteran, Gary attended Evansville University. In 1968 he relocated to Erie County, Ohio as hog buyer for the Waldock Meat Packing Company. When that factory closed he entered into real estate, a career that would last forty years. It was also in 1968 that he met and married Dona, his companion for fifty-three years, until her death in 2022.

Father of Jenny and Buck, grandfather of C.J. and Cassie, Gary continues to remember the years among the cowboys, traders and feed lots. He passes these tales on whenever he finds someone to listen.

BOOKS BY BIRD DOG PUBLISHING

Travis, Texas by Gary Harmon, 218 pgs, $18
Road Kill by R. J. Norgard, 346 pgs, $18
Inside the Flow by Nancy Dunham, 62 pgs. $15
Lost and Found in Alaska by Joel D. Rudinger, 242 pgs. $18
Mingo Town & Memories by Larry Smith, 96 pgs. $15
Trophy Kill by R. J. Norgard, 256 pgs. $16
Symphonia Judaica: Jewish Symphony and Other Poems
by Joel D. Rudinger, 117 pgs. $16
Words Walk: Poems by Ronald M. Ruble, 168 pgs. $16
Homegoing by Michael Olin-Hitt, 180 pgs. $16
A Wonderful Stupid Man: Stories by Allen Frost, 190 pgs. $16
A Poetic Journey, Poems by Robert A. Reynolds, 86 pgs. $16
Dogs and Other Poems by Paul Piper, 80 pgs. $15
The Mermaid Translation by Allen Frost, 140 pgs. $15
Heart Murmurs: Poems by John Vanek, 120 pgs. $15
Home Recordings: Tales and Poems by Allen Frost, $14
A Life in Poems by William C. Wright, $10
Faces and Voices: Tales by Larry Smith, 136 pgs. $14
Second Story Woman: A Memoir of Second Chances
by Carole Calladine, 226 pgs. $15
256 Zones of Gray: Poems by Rob Smith, 80 pgs. $14
Another Life: Collected Poems by Allen Frost, 176 pgs. $14
Winter Apples: Poems by Paul S. Piper, 88 pgs. $14
Lake Effect: Poems by Laura Treacy Bentley, 108 pgs. $14
Depression Days on an Appalachian Farm: Poems
by Robert L. Tener, 80 pgs. $14
*120 Charles Street, The Village: Journals & Other Writings
1949-1950* by Holly Beye, 240 pgs. $15

An Imprint of Bottom Dog Press, Inc.
P.O. Box 425 /Huron, Ohio 44839
http://smithdocs.net